ROTTEN ROW

Angela Hargreaves

ISBN-13: 978-1-47938–611-6

The story of ROTTEN ROW touches on periods from the nineteen fifties through to the present time and contains tales of love, death, nostalgic regret, sexual encounters, romance, marriage, divorce and desperate times but ultimately how quickly our fortunes can and do change.

Rotten Row is about the petty spitefulness and complexity of living in close proximity to some neighbours.

To describe the phenomenon that is precisely community with adjoining territories

I quote Sigmund Freud,

"The narcissism of minor differences."

This appropriately sums up ROTTEN ROW. It is a concatenation of all things.

Threads that are joined together through accident of time or place.

However, the characters in ROTTEN ROW are fictional and many of the things that happen in the book didn't happen at all.

I made them up or stole them from the lives of other people that I've met over the years.

All have been hugely exaggerated for comic or tragic effect.

I had a 'I'll use this someday file' and hoped to one day take advantage of what seemed to me to be a collection of just the sort of comic slightly public episodes that was destined to be used by someone sooner rather than later.

My fictitious characters live in the fictional village of Upton Green.

Always remember that the cave you fear to enter holds the treasure you seek.

Joseph Campbell

ABOUT THE AUTHOR

Angela Hargreaves was born in Lichfield Staffordshire but relocated to Twickenham aged eighteen, followed by moves to Highgate N6 and then to Hampshire for some country living.

On returning to Staffordshire, she worked as an administrator for a children's charity.

She has three grown up stepsons and lives between Staffordshire and Devon with her husband and two little dogs.

Interests and work now merge, as they are interior design, house renovation and gardening.

ACKNOWLEDGMENTS

I would like to express my thanks to Carol and Toni Russ for their help and encouragement with this book

.

CONTENTS

CHAPTER 1

Death Row and Upton Green Village

Deprived of vigour, once again returning from another amble past death row with the nauseating stench of shit in my lungs and thoughts of all those horrid bright orange and bloated flies chomping away on the seemingly endless cowpats.

The second walk of the day completed, through the churchyard, past the long line of cremation stones and into one of two meadows, Town and Church. Today it was the Town Meadow for a stroll through the fertilizer pong and cow dung. Such are the delights of country living. I was convinced it was going to be all floaty dresses and trugs full of flowers.

Once upon a time in another life I was friends with a Friesian cow. I used to feed her cattle nuts from a bucket, but even before I took it upon myself to feed her treats, she would follow me as I walked with my elderly dog Levi and my then young dogs, Elvira and Blythe.

Matty, as I called my black and white companion would cleverly and expertly limbo under barbed wire fences that blocked her way to walk just a little behind us along the water's edge of a bird watching nature reserve for which I had keys to the gates that opened over onto cattle grids.

1

Angela Hargreaves

hardly ever met anyone, which was probably a good thing, as we must have looked a strange sight.

Matty was big, beautiful and blooming. I loved her rough tongue when I let her lick my hands. Her long angular face that I often wished I could draw, instead I took lots of photographs. Her huge brown eyes with long, long lashes were placid and unperturbed pools of serenity.

Sometimes I would drive along the narrow parkland road that went through the middle of her fields and she would leave the other cows and run alongside my car.

I've never really been a country girl though I have had three attempts in different parts of rural England, but I loved this relationship with my bovine friend and I thought of her as mine, my special friend. I loved her. It could only end in tears and it did, buckets of them where the nuts used to be.

Forever I shall carry with me my own sad cow story.

A small herd of Friesian cattle arrived a few at a time in the back of a horsebox onto the private parkland at the back of my then marital home. There was nothing unusual about this except that it was on the very day that I had asked my husband for a divorce and when I went for a walk taking care to stay away from the cows and not awaken their curiosity when one of our new neighbours took it upon herself to amble gently across to us. The dogs weren't at all worried, I put my hand out to her palm side up, and she licked it. I was crying, still upset with the row I'd just escaped from but more out of relief in getting things out in the open than anything else. I felt I'd jumped off a mad roller coaster of emotions having finally come to a definite decision.

I was amazed when I saw her easily slip under a barbed wire fence and continue with us on our walk. When I stopped, she stopped. I sat on a fence and she

2

let me stroke her head.

It was inevitable that at some point I was going to have a run in with the farmer for taking one of his cows on daily walks. One day she was out with us when he came to do his check on the herd. A Land Rover came to an abrupt halt a few yards away from us and a rather short but good-looking man got out and walked very purposefully towards us.

I liked what I saw but thought it could go one of two ways. He was either going to be angry or understanding and see my point of view. Fortunately, it was the latter.

He started to turn up at our walk times and join us on our walks.

Within a couple of weeks we were having pleasant romps in the back of his horse box or in little woods as the dogs munched on biscuits they were bribed with and Matty grazed contentedly.

I was honest from the outset; our relationship was to be for pleasure, a few afternoons of fun.

This was good for a while. I learnt a little bit about farming but my main concern was Matty's future. In fact, Matty and Maud's future to be precise. As the months passed I realised that Matty had a friend who was quite dependant on her. When Matty wasn't on one of her walks Maud was always with her. This small herd of cattle had been born around the same time on the same farm and reared together. They were brought on and when old enough artificially inseminated and whilst in calf were sold at market. Matty and Maud were in calf and due to go to market.

I was broke, hardly earning enough to support myself and my dogs due to going through a horrible separation and funding divorce proceedings.

How could I buy two cows at the then going rate of several hundred pounds each and then keep them plus what of their calves?

By this point the novelty of afternoon romps had worn off and I was rather bored with Mr. Farmer who, it has to be said, really did try very hard to please, obviously to make up for his lack of stature.

Apparently, Meningitis as a child was responsible for him being very short. It didn't explain his possessive little temper tantrums and insular personality. Basically, he turned out to be rather dull. Another reason to want to leave the marital pile. I pleaded with him not to sell Matty or Maud, but he said there was no way he was going to milk two cows or indeed keep two cows that would fetch good money.

Eventually we did a deal; a very unsatisfactory one. Matty was to be sold to another dairy farmer in a private sale locally and poor Maud was going to market where a better price was likely. The day came to separate Matty and Maud and to put Maud into the horsebox to be taken to market. It was awful, she really fought against it. Matty stood there watching, still and silent as Maud made gut wrenching noises and was eventually pushed up the ramp with no way out.

I walked away and cried and Maddy followed me.

I would drive my old car along the private road between the fields and she would run alongside.

The following week the horsebox came for Matty. I wasn't told when so I wasn't there. I was asked not to visit here on her new farm to let her settle. I used to drive by to see if I could see her. I wrote to the farmer and asked him to take good care of Matty and if ever my situation changed, would he let me buy her back? He was a kind man and invited me to see her. I was early and arrived to see her being hosed down.

She looked miserable. I went to her and she never looked at me and didn't respond to my voice. Her spirit was broken and so was mine. Not long afterwards, I rang again to see how she was. I couldn't forget her. I was told she had died the night before of a twisted stomach. She had given birth to a female calf prior to this that was doing well.

I cannot bear to look at Friesian cows or their paintings in galleries. I have kept Matty's photographs but I couldn't look at them not even now. I felt I'd betrayed her and had so totally let her down.

There was no need to continue with Mr Farmer and I told him so, quite gently I hope.

Sadly, the ego was bigger than the man was and he made a horrible public fuss that further complicated legal matters.

He also put a large dead rat on the bonnet of my car and watched from a distance whilst I discovered it in the murky half-light of an early morning.

He was a mean spirited licentious gnome who required the sort of personal growth not found on a farmyard.

We live and learn though it is usually exhausting, expensive, irretrievable and too late.

This is my story of an ordinary life in a quintessential middle England country village and my escape from that typified rural idyll, but not before my experiences of village life become entwined with those of other locals, not least the eclectic inhabitants of 'Rotten Row' and other characters.

Rural seasons are as follows: In early spring, no one can never quite escape the all pervading, cloying smell of muck-spreading that wafts from fields near and far.

Summer, there are flies, lots of flies. Autumn, much rotting vegetation and mud.

Winter. Mud and scenic snow. The church paths

always ice over so walks are hazardous and that is when I let Blythe and Elvira run free whilst I stumble and slip whilst clinging onto the gravestones like Lady Deadlock from Bleak House looking for the pauper's grave of her dead lover. Reaching the kissing gate that leads into the meadows always feels like a massive achievement.

The village is Upton Green and my name is Louisa. The location is not quite 'Straw Dogs' territory, being not too far off the beaten track but nonetheless, rural.

Four times each day, I walk to and fro through the churchyard with my two small dogs, Elvira and Blythe, from our home at Blackbird Cottage.

My little dogs dash about and thoughts run amok in my head. Friends and demons.

The old grave stones don't bother me so much, they have their own kind of beauty, lichen growing over ghostly letters and all manner of shapes, some grand, some flat slabs of stone, together with the odd crumbling sepulchre.

I did once ask the vicar why gravestones were generally inscribed on the east face.

Apparently, this has been the case for more than a century and Christians in this green and pleasant land have always been buried on an east-west alignment with feet pointing to the east. Early gravestones were placed at the head end with the inscription on the west face, that is, facing away from the grave. Late 18th-century and early 19th-century graves often also had footstones. The footstones were usually much smaller than the headstone and were inscribed on the east face, once more facing outwards from the grave. Inscriptions were minimal and usually limited to initials and year of death, for example B.H.1863. A fact stuck in the jumble of my head for all eternity with loads of others, as that was the year the London Underground was opened.

Sometime around 1860 kerbs were introduced and the footstone dispensed with and the head stone turned around with the inscription on the inside, facing the grave.

Those were the days, of carved angels and so on with beautiful script, as was the stonemason's art. Now gravestones are all much the same. Mediocrity lives on after death.

Highgate cemetery is an inspirational place to visit. A timeless gatherer of remains, an ethereal haven. I have always found a visit there takes away all fears of death or living. But hey, back to my local dead neighbours.

The volunteers who laboriously tend the churchyard speak of the dead inhabitants as if they were residing in suburban streets. I often hear them call to each other.

"Oh yes, I've cut the grass and weeded as far as Mr Higgins and I'm on my way to start at Mrs Peakes."

It's as if Mrs Peakes was about to put the kettle on.

There is a very old double headstone where the script on one half tells of a husband who will wait on the other side for his wife to join him in eternity. Alas, she didn't and her share of the stone remains blank. I like to make stories up in my head for this one. My everyday elegy for the dead is ever changing.

CHAPTER 2

Husbands, Lovers and Conception.

It is an impressive plot and a sizeable piece of stone, so maybe the errant wife lived on a large country farm, two a penny in this neck of the woods. Finding life as a widow too much to bear and children too troublesome to tolerate anymore, she simply sold the estate and ran off with the gamekeeper, leaving the children with a relative.

My former mother-in-law Isobel did a similar thing, only she was still married to a farmer by the name of Henry when she bolted with Willy their gamekeeper and general help. Together Isobel and Henry had produced five children in quick succession, two girls and three boys whilst living at their farm.

Willy was a huge man with hands the width of tennis rackets. Few people knew that he had the much more romantic name of Gabriel Studwick. Rather appropriate all things considered, since he was Isobel's lover and the pair of them running away together, leaving Henry to bring up the children.

Isobel and Willy lived together amongst hundreds of pheasants, smelly ferrets and many compliant working dogs in a rundown but idyllic thatched cottage in deepest Hampshire countryside until they each died of old age, within weeks of each other.

Dear Henry, a charming man, outlived them by a decade, cherished and adored by his children, as was their mother; it has to be said, before a cruel illness took him to his death. An era over.

My former husband, 'The Prince of Darkness', not affectionately known as POD for short, was not one of Henry's sons. He was Isobel's illegitimate baby born before Henry and Isobel were married. A moment of passion during the war, conceived some time during nineteen forty three in a churchyard during crepuscular moments. That much of the story Isobel divulged. Whether she could not actually remember who the father was, or maybe she was protecting his identity we shall never know. She hinted that paternity possibly belonged to an American airman; personally, I think the father was probably Count Dracula, because Isobel's illegitimate son certainly drained me of practically every drop of my energy, though not quite all of my spirit, the bastard, and I say that most literally.

I first met Isobel on a beautiful summer's day in her garden, which was abundant with flowers, a riot of colour and scent. She had a little Jack Russell dog at her feet. Isobel had the same pale blue eyes as her illegitimate son, but hers twinkled, the same shape of mouth but hers was kinder and her blonde hair was gently waved in the style of a nineteen forties starlet. It was strong luxurious hair just like her son's, but his was dark, very dark.

This was his second meeting with his mother. The first had been arranged carefully by Isobel and Henry's eldest daughter and took place over tea at The Ritz. It was an emotional affair and Isobel said she'd always hoped to find her baby boy one day. Isobel was found after my 'Prince of Darkness's' widowed, adopted father had died. I'm glad I didn't meet his adopted mother, Hilda, because quite frankly she sounded horrible. I was told that she was a very neat woman, large and bovine. Spoons had to be laid upon her sink draining board scoop side down. Her china was pearlised blue, the glaze resembling an oil slick. I know this because I lived with some of the ghastly stuff for years.

When she and Cyril (adopted father) took delivery of their adopted baby, he was, it is said, so clean he was almost polished, with not a strand of baby hair out of place and paraded around in a gleaming pram from 'The Prestige Baby Emporium'. At the time, Cyril owned a little Jack Russell terrier called Scamp. Scamp took to sitting at the side of the pram and was as gentle as a lamb when the baby was put on the floor. Wherever the baby went, Scamp was beside the pram. One afternoon whilst Cyril was at work Hilda had a visit from one of her corseted friends. It was a summer's afternoon and they were having tea on the lawn whilst the baby slept in his pram with Scamp snoozing alongside. The friend commented on the dog being by the pram and Hilda said how much Scamp seemed to protect the baby. The friend said, "You want to be careful, one day he'll turn on the baby, they get jealous you know."

Later that same afternoon before Cyril returned from his work Hilda took Scamp to the vet and had him put to sleep.

What price loyalty?

'Oh, for the touch of a vanished paw or the sound of a voice that is still'.

Horrid Hilda.

On discovering what Hilda had done Cyril was devastated and furious and began to dislike the baby who was, subsequently, due to no fault of his own, disapproved of and disciplined as soon as he began to walk, by a strict authoritarian father and fussed over by an overbearing, needy mother. It was not a fun household.

It was a relief when a scholarship was won and the child went off to boarding school.

However, humour and optimism are transcendent.

They have to be.

All's over, then does truth sound bitter
As one at first believes?
Hark 'tiss the sparrows' good night twitter
About your cottage eaves!

(Robert Browning)

Strangely, years later we have been in contact, just the odd email, communications over the ether. None the less, it feels that all those years were not wasted if something can be salvaged from them, though the 'Prince of Darkness' will always be a selfish and opinionated old git.

Shared history, time and memories not least of the dogs that we have shared and loved until the end of their all too short lives, and the associated people of that period that I really liked will always be there as distant friends.

However, I digress with thoughts, opinions and the many conversations that go on quite independently in my head and let us return to the tombstones of Upton Green.

CHAPTER 3

Parenthood, Brothers and Wives

On another. Sweet are the memories that never fade.

Not so, I would erase so many troublesome ones of mine for I am tormented with regret and angst about all sorts of things that can never be changed.

Who isn't? Guilt is an expensive commodity.

Returning to the subject of parentage. As a child often, I wished that I had been adopted. I was never my mother's daughter. Oh, to be relieved of that source of discomfiture. Children embarrass easily and I was no exception. Mostly it was ignorance. These days my late mother's behaviour would have a name. Learning disabilities probably, but then I didn't understand.

My mother, Rosa, would walk around the house naked; have tantrums or spells of quiet, not speaking for weeks. The family diet was not good even by nineteen fifties standards. The shopping list consisted of chocolate, lots of biscuits, usually bags of broken ones from Woolworth's. It wasn't until I left home that I realised they could be bought whole! Lots of greasy chips and white hollow cobs full of air, vegetables so over cooked they were a mush. Sprouts were served flat! Generally the shaping of food as she put it, was a nuisance, it made a mess and interrupted her obsessional cleaning and furniture moving.

My mother was so house proud she polished shadows. Nothing was ever in the same place, with the exception of the worshipped television set. We had new second hand furniture regularly and my poor dad decorated rooms as often as he was instructed. We had murals on all four walls of the sitting room once, you could be by a lake, at the top of a snow-capped mountain, walking through forests or be on a boat on the Med all at the same time.

It wasn't wise to get attached to a particular toy, jigsaw or book as they were all just dust collectors and would be disposed of as soon as the owner was out of sight. As a compromise, I started to hoard clear polythene bags and covered my teddies and dolls up. My little girl's room looked like a crime scene of bagged bodies.

I was a mousey quiet child, with a jagged fringe and thin ponytail, much maligned by Rosa for not having thick curly hair and for looking like dad. Onion Head is what she called me, because as a baby I had a few wispy strands of hair right in the middle of an otherwise bald head. I can't say things improved much as I got older, except I didn't look like an onion any longer. Basically, I was just hoping not to be noticed, always pulling skirts and dresses over my knees and was never without a buttoned up cardie even on the hottest of days.

It was a lonely childhood and my friends were books and my salvation the library. Because I read 'older' books, my vocabulary and speech sometimes came across as if from past decades and perhaps still does.

My world of literature was kinder than the one I existed in. I would imagine my own home and look forward to the day I escaped. As granny had suggested, my suitcase was always packed and ready, if only metaphorically. My mother's household was as

15

mad, twisted and lacking in any warmth or creativity as her jumbled head. Nylon sheets and crimplene clothes were invented for my mother, they didn't move or crease. Our house was so static we could have generated our own electricity. On one occasion, she said that she wanted a split-level oven so told dad to cut the grill off the one we had.

She was at all times contrary and inconsistent. Her body language would be overtly sexual whilst verbally declaring sex to be a dirty business. On giving a gift, she would say, "But don't tell anyone, especially your father because he wouldn't want you to have it." If another child's mother asked if I wanted to go for tea she'd say how nice it was to be asked and thanks and so on and then say to me, "You don't want to go there, they're dirty people with filthy crockery." Hence even if I went I was frightened to eat anything. Eventually people gave up all except my dad who loved her to death, his, literally. He repeatedly forgave how horrible she was to him, the violence, all the times she hit him and there were many. He even coped very well with her wandering off with other men. She was beautiful to look at, childlike, vindictive, vulnerable, vain, uneducated and desperately unstable. Rosa loved Rosa and adored her reflection in mirrors.

I don't think he ever regretted taking her in and marrying her straight from the sanatorium where she had been for a couple of years suffering from tuberculosis. Her family didn't want her back. They openly said she was too difficult, unemployable and even madder on a full moon. Nonetheless, she had looked radiant on her wedding day in a beautiful borrowed wedding dress. Dad cancelled his ballroom dancing exam scheduled for that day and never danced again except with me, as a child standing on his feet. To this day when I dance with a partner, I have to lead! The dancing gene wasn't passed down. I still stand on feet!

They started their married life living with my dad's parents, Agatha and her third husband Jo. It was said it was Agatha's revolting cooking that killed the first two husbands off, mould being a regular ingredient. However, it was more likely to be the First World War, but I never found out. Agatha was a strict authoritarian. A difficult, handsome, religious woman. She wore full cross over aprons in dowdy patterns with a small bible in one pocket and a flask of whisky in another. Her long grey hair was scraped into a tight little bun. To my child's eye Agatha resembled the Russian mother doll that held all the smaller ones but without the benign smile and none of the colour.

She had two other sons as well as my dad, but I seldom saw them, as they didn't visit.

Agatha had a daughter too, who dropped by occasionally, though she was mentally unstable since the death of her little boy in a drowning accident.

My dad was a tattoo artist at night and at weekends, working from the garden shed, where a gentle but persistent whirring noise could be heard, this was before the days of health and safety. He was good at it though and was frequently busy and when he wasn't with customers, he was designing his own tattoos. During the day, he would go out decorating.

The days were particularly awful, as Agatha had hated Rosa on sight. On one occasion, there was an almighty row because Agatha had thrown Rosa's engagement ring into the fire. Rosa had put it on the mantelpiece for safe keeping one washday Monday and returned to find it thrown into the flames. That night Rosa and dad left in his green Morris Minor 999LRF (I've always remembered the car registration) and found a house to rent. Agatha and Jo were neither visited or spoken to again by Rosa for some considerable time, not until I was about two years old, when I was taken there by dad occasionally, for them to mind me.

Rosa had bitten my ears a few times and said it was because I was naughty, so in the interests of me having ears and as strict and joyless as Agatha was she tolerated me. Jo, my grandfather was fun. He made a rustic wooden swing for me that these days would never get past health and safety and we spent hours down the bottom of the long and overgrown garden, avoiding Agatha, eating sweets and dreading meal times. Jo died suddenly, Agatha got sick and we never visited her in hospital. I overheard compassionless conversations that told of her toes dropping off because of gangrene

Our lives went on much the same.

Many years later after my father's cruel and horrible fight with cancer ended, I left the care of our mother to my brother on the basis that I'd left home at fifteen, so he knew her better.

So terrified was I of being left with her to look after, I wrote to her doctors, stating that I would never consider such an ordeal, so therefore I was not an option. I last saw her through her letterbox. She was in her house, I'd called to tend the garden, and I couldn't operate the key pad that unlocked the door. Her Alzheimer's was so advanced she was not capable of doing anything except for escaping and wandering the streets, hence the lock.

Obviously, this wasn't acceptable and eventually she was taken into full time care, which was a great relief. My brother and his most recent, cold and efficient wife dealt with everything and I was happy for them to do it. I blamed my mother for not even sharing the grief of dad's death when I should have been glad of it. I couldn't escape the frustration of the past to adequately deal with the present. It was a truly awful, raw time. A needy mother can produce an emotionally cold child, just like a bossy parent sometimes creates a child who is incapable of making a decision without first seeking permission.

I never saw my mother again. Was this learned behaviour, first Agatha and now Rosa? What goes around comes around. I remember how she would delegate what should have been adult tasks. I know it sounds dramatic but I was robbed of my childhood.

ROTTEN ROW

My mother was the child.

She would dictate her letters to me and greeting card writing and remembering special dates was always my job. She could write, she just didn't want to do anything that couldn't be delegated. I never saw her read a book. Strangely, she was good at figures, managed money well but sometimes, although she had it, she couldn't bear to part with it and this is what caused a lot of rows. Packets of money were squirreled away all over the house and still there were days when my brother and I were instructed to hide behind the sofa so that the rent man couldn't see us when he called. Sometimes it was the same with the local grocery shop run by a miserable old woman called Hilda Talbot. When she wasn't paid at the end of the week, it wasn't wise to go into the shop for sweets or there would be questions and demands.

I wonder sometimes why she didn't hold us for ransom.

It was a shilling for the meter existence. I remember taking jumpers and tops off last as I slid into the long enamel bath. The tall walls and small frosted window panes running with condensation. Baths were always a speedy affair as the water went cold very quickly. It was only a once a week experience. Hair washing was done over the kitchen sink with a jug, tears and tangles.

We had few visitors, as sometimes Rosa could be unforgivably rude to neighbours and family. Or worse, crushingly embarrassing. My dad did have friends away from the house but sometimes he would pay for his little bit of pleasure as Rosa was wont to hide behind the garden gate and hit him when he arrived home. This would be followed by a raging tantrum and at least three weeks of broody silence. There was an epic silence that was maintained for most of her pregnancy with my younger brother. He was born at home, as was normal in those days, but he was a sickly baby and tensions were high.

He was a sweet baby who grew into an adorable toddler, despite having had sand thrown in his eyes by another child whilst they were playing. This resulted in eye infections, perhaps related, I'm not sure, and those little round NHS glasses. He learnt self-preservation very quickly and also after a sizzling experience, not to pick up hot coals from the fire and was quite a responsible little boy. We both had spots and rotten teeth due to our bad diets.

Our expectations were low, though we neither of us managed them well. I left home at age fifteen and fell into the predictable pitfalls of promiscuity and alcohol, in pursuit of an antidote for feelings of inadequacy, engendered by the general shortcomings of a life that I believed to be normal. Meanwhile my brother looked for security in girlfriends, who strangely looked like a younger sane version of our mother. They were usually pretty but empty-headed girls. Also, a career in sport eluded him when he badly injured one of his knees. The only light on his horizon, dashed. He had a talent for drawing but no one paid much attention to a tool that could have earned him a living. He just gave up, disillusioned and not knowing where to turn. It's hard living without encouragement, inspiration or enthusiasm, each day being much the same and so few expectations.

I think the knee injury was the last straw and one day our dad found him in a bath of blood. He'd cut his wrists. My brother survived but an all-pervading sense of despair encompassed dad. One day I found him standing at a bus stop just crying, saying he couldn't take any more and I didn't know what to say. All this was brought back to me when I saw a small teddy encased in polythene on one of the cremation stones, obviously as protection against the weather, but it sent a chill right up my spine.

And now, as is often the case on these maudlin walks, I can't shake the demons from my shoulders.

Just a few years ago, my brother was rescued like a dog from a home, by a woman more than a decade older than himself, divorced, wealthy, capable and comfortable in a beige suburban bubble, whom he married. She arranged everything and all he had to do was put on the suit that had been packed for him when they were on holiday in New Zealand for their wedding. She did however take obsessive care of him to the exclusion of everyone else. A bargain. She was rich and he was handsome and young.

Did I mention that when the spots had cleared up and with some dental work done, that my little brother was a good looking man with very little self worth since first marrying a thoroughly manipulative and lazy, drunken version of our mother, though not in looks. I didn't discover until he'd left his first wife that he'd been working all day in a mediocre job to go home to mental and physical abuse, so bad that he often slept in his car in the garage. This to avoid being bashed about the body with bottles and ashtrays by a woman so warped and who had been, at one point literally wired up in the local mental institution, St. James's.

Like father, like son. Victims.

Dear Lauren, the first wife, what a woman she was! Not unlike John Everett Millais's 'Ophelia' to look at, she too was often to be found horizontal and very pale.

If the painting of 'Ophelia' floating in the water was stood on end, that would be Lauren. Pale skin, long red hair and a vacant expression. The only thing Lauren was interested in was, oddly, vitamin pills by the sack full, cosmetics by the truckload and American gangster movies on video, washed down with vats of alcohol and Benson & Hedges cigarettes. She also, quite alarmingly, had a subscription to Real Life Crime magazine.

Lauren became pregnant quite early in their relationship. Having never worked, there was little change except for the quantities of shopping hauled home on the bus and left unpacked, enough to stock shops. There was no sex after conception just lots of abuse. The house was filthy, no money for food that wasn't in a take away box. Then there was the birth of a baby girl and bankruptcy. The baby was taken in by Laurens parents and my brother left. There was a divorce and years of maintenance to come. The baby girl was a picture of her mother. Attempts were made regarding her education and upbringing but they were not wanted. All that was required were the regular child support payments. Fortunately, the maintenance stopped when the child reached sixteen, as she did not want to continue her education. Within months she was living in a squat, selling drugs and pregnant. Learnt behaviour. What goes around comes around.

But back to my brother's present-day life with his second wife.

After our mothers poorly attended funeral they moved to France without leaving a forwarding address and I don't expect to hear from them again. So I'm truly an orphan. In many ways, life is better but there are times when I feel like a rug has been pulled from beneath my feet. I see their faces in my head and I want to shout I'm sorry, at the top of my voice, sorry for everything, even the stuff that I could not have helped. The problem is the responsibility that I still feel, no matter what, because I didn't make things better for my dad or my brother.

Ah well, what is done is done.

I say my life is better, not because I ever wished my parents dead; I just didn't want to be that child, their child. Grandma Agatha gave me a little brown suitcase to keep, that she said I should pack some of my things in and be ready because the best place for me would be Dr. Barnardo's Children's Home. She was right, maybe it would have been. What with the suitcase and her tales of her tabby cat who turned into a tiger at night time, ready to eat any child not in bed by six o'clock.

The cat's shadow was a terrifying sight, especially when seen through thin unlined bedroom curtains. In fact, the cat was a miserable and aloof feline, just like

Granma.

I still see Granma's face as clear as clear and Grandpa's but the problems started later than the period when I knew them.

The past should stay in the past. It's like they are all in a sepia photograph, one by one slowly disappearing.

I have on occasion had some counselling sessions to help alleviate the stupid feelings of guilt that I sometimes have and it was at one of these meetings that I was advised to write the following letter that did help me to move on and be at peace with myself as much as anyone ever can be.

Good karma is very important, guilt being so expensive.

The Letter:

To My Mother,

From the child that was to the woman that is,
goodbye to you, finally goodbye.
Goodbye to the guilt, embarrassment and insecurity.
Free from the curse of cynicism. I am my own
person, I love, I care and I wish people joy in their
lives.
And for myself, let the healing begin.

To my Father,

Wherever you are, I hope you are happy and at
peace.
I always wanted so much for you. You had the
skills to do the things that would have brought you
contentment. I remember trying to encourage you,

but I was the 'child' it was not for me to do.
I loved your humour and the way you used to dance
about the house or pretend to be a male model on a
catwalk and a very camp one at that.
You were evasive and seldom consistent, telling
people what they wanted to hear, rather than face
debate or conflict. The easy option.
I did not admire that trait in you or the spiteful
attitude you sometimes had. Though I know this
was out of frustration.
I loved you and I think you loved me. And no one
will ever make me laugh like you did. There will
never ever be another you.
Ours was a confusing relationship. You told me once
that you were thinking of leaving and on another
occasion that you were considering taking your own
life.
Love and despair.
What was I supposed to say or do? I was so young.
I left, you stayed and you loved my mother as you
always had. It was, I guess, the one thing that you
were consistent about and perhaps the very one
you should not have been. Love and dogged loyalty
took what could have been from you.
I don't think of you so much now. There is no need
to revisit the scene.
The conflict of grief and guilt has gone.
You were you and I am me.
Goodbye. I am moving on without you in my life.
The healing must begin.

ROTTEN ROW

To my brother.

*You have moved on and gave me no address or
number.*
*I know the divide was too much. The gap of
experiences too wide to fill.*
*We lost each other years ago, but still I remember
your baby photographs in my head.*
*To cut all ties, sometimes that's how it's meant to
be.*
*Be happy, love, be loved and I wish you good health
and contentment.*

To my brother's wife,

*The experience of knowing you was painful and
arduous.*
You have the same beady eyes as my mother.
*Like hers, they are not kind. I hope you will be good
to my brother and because of this, I wish you the
best in all you do.*
Goodbye.

Let the healing begin.

In other words, I just picked myself up and got on
with life, just like everyone else.

It's not where you come from but what you make of
yourself.

In some cases neither nature nor nurture.

Change your thoughts, change your actions,
change your life became my mantra.

I don't believe my upbringing was that bad, just typical for children raised in the 1950's, a rather brutal, intolerant, spiritual void.

Having recently read and seen the television adaptation of Nigel Slater's 'Toast', I would have welcomed Nigel's stepmother, Mrs Potter. From a food aspect, every day was a banquet!

Why didn't Mr Slater senior just buy her a café and rake in the profit?

I wonder what ever happened to Mrs. Potter? Stepmothers and stepfathers have a difficult time. I think a parent will always love their child in a special way above anyone else whereas a child will love others more than the parent, so a stepparent will always be placed after their loved ones child. It's just how it is. It would be impractical to surmise otherwise.

But again, I deviate, and ramble away from the churchyard on an entirely different tangent.

Conversations in my head again.

It's the mediocre crematorium squares of lacklustre, almost cheap kitchen work surface marble that gets to me most. They are a motley ditch brown colour. A gloom descends every time I pass by, what I call death row and invariably makes me question my own mortality, how average I am, and my own worth. And things too late for reparation. It is often said that we live and learn but all too often, the lesson is too late to be of any use. Oh to have the wisdom to live in the moment. Of the crematorium stones there is just one that I like, it simply states Lily Allen 1900-1987 and nothing else.

Its simplicity is intriguing. When new ones are added, I feel sad and worry about when it will be me, not that I want to be buried anywhere but fleetingly I share in the grief of the bereaved. Usually strangers, but worse when I recognise them. It can't be helped, their sorrow grabs me as I walk on past and it clings like gossamer spider webs.

These days death row has metamorphosed into a semi-detached suburbia of resplendent plastic miniature boundaries and an abundance of gaudy plastic blooms in all manner of household pots. High visibility chrysanthemums! Some have escaped this, but far too many, showing human nature at its gaudy best have achieved what Vera Duckworth did in Coronation Street and plenty of other people have done to spoil a row of terrace houses with their choice of colourful cladding and plastic windows and doors to spoil the integrity of an honest house.

I know fresh blooms can be prohibitively expensive and that plastic lasts through at least a year of absent visits, but I can't help think that less is definitely more.

Maintenance could be sheep or goats, chomp, chomp, chomping away, and the hard working volunteers could go out and have a fun time.

Mourners have procured double their deceased allotted space, claiming proprietary by edging the acquired boundary with corrugated strips of green plastic or orange stained planks.

Even mini hedges. The mentality of suburbia lives on.

There are plastic squirrels, robins, and chipped novelty teapots with smiley bears.

Shrines. I simply can't bear the futile feelings that I have been experiencing of late so Death Row was quite high on my list of Reasons to Leave Upton Green Village

Angela Hargreaves

Move along these shades
In gentleness of heart
With gentle hand
Touch for there is spirit in the woods

(William Wordsworth)

CHAPTER 4

The Protean Church.

Whilst on the subject of the churchyard there have been many happy occasions to view. I have, over the years seen lots of weddings and it must be said some guests have needed help and silently I have obliged. The temptation to shout out, suppressed.

Countless price tickets to be viewed on the visible rise on the soles of outrageously high heels as their owners clatter under the lych-gate and totter up the path to the church like over dressed drunks. Then there are the visible panty lines and streaked fake tans. Clothes so stiff they wear their owners and could probably walk on their own, topped with stiff meringue hats that have to be held because they don't sit properly. Why is it that the most important of outfits can go horribly wrong? Trying too hard probably. At my own wedding, it is true; I resembled a crinoline lady loo roll cover. However, here at St Augustine's it was mostly beautiful brides, happy guests, and interesting cars. Camper vans, double-decker buses and all manner of classic cars.

The theatre of life, christenings, weddings and funerals are all regularly played out before my windows like the best bits of a soap opera or reality television.

There is a downside, the church bells are

maddeningly loud living so near to the church and it's always best to be out on the nights the bell ringers' practice and I certainly thought it wise to not allow prospective buyer viewings on Monday nights clanging sessions. I can honestly say that in the ten years that I have lived at Black Bird Cottage the local campanologists have improved little and variations of ringing have been nonexistent.

For whom the bell tolls!

Bloody bells. Noisy Christians.

The vicar has a very necessary sense of humour and a charming vagueness that regularly saves him from the wrath of the ladies of the flower guild.

A bossy, gossipy, hissy, humourless, competitive bunch of Hyacinth Bucket's that anyone could wish not to encounter.

Heaven help the poor bride to be who doesn't comply with their wishes when organising wedding flowers for the church.

I once heard them say to a new member of their coven, who was enquiring what the correct protocol was for all things church related and they replied with an ear piercing cackle that the vicar, Charles, just does as he's told.

CHAPTER 5

Charles, Elspeth and Matthew

On seeing him in the churchyard one morning I said, "Morning Charles."

He wittily replied, "No I'm just walking the dogs!"

A quick play on words for such an early hour.

He likes to show people his many clerical garments that hang in a closet housed in a cool stone room that smells of incense and polish.

Charles is a kind family man, knowledgeable on many subjects. His wife, Elspeth, is a force to be reckoned with. A woman of many sides and all of them characterful or just mad. Oddly demonic, a woman possessed. Elspeth is all things, infuriating, exasperating and just when you think that throttling her would be a good option she'll do or say something amazingly intuitive or kind. Never have I come across a more harassed Christian. Elspeth runs everywhere with the great lolloping gait of a very large puppy. Her very good clothes always a size too small, handbags that are stuffed with more rubbish than your average wheelie bin. Elspeth and Charles have four grown up children who would not look out of place in a Burberry advertisement they are so naturally stylish and attractive.

Really beautiful young people. How this happened no one knows.

It was spitefully said that their beautiful genes must come from Charles's line.

Mathew

I once met one of their two sons in the waiting room of the Cognitive Behaviour Councillor I was seeing. What a coincidence that was as I thought I'd chosen one far enough away not to see anyone I knew. I picked up the obligatory Country Life but soon found myself giggling behind its glossy pages as I couldn't help but overhear something funny.

Our conversation began because he was talking to a friend on his mobile phone bemoaning his mother's stupidity of washing wool on a hot wash. The jumper he was almost wearing resembled boiled felt. "Everything, bloody everything is washed on hot. Grandma bought mom a Paul Smith dress, jacket, skirt and top for her birthday, they were really expensive and the whole lot went in a hot wash. Gran went mad!"

Hence, this explained most of Elspeth's clothes being too small. We started to talk because I couldn't help but laugh at the overheard conversation.

It turned out that Matthew was there because he was struggling with being gay. Or his mother was struggling with the reality of it. Elspeth was not accepting Matthew's sexuality because of her faith. It really should have been Elspeth at the counselling session not the young man.

Charles seemed to be a lot more accommodating than his wife. I was finding him to be most sagacious. Poor Matthew struggled and went through a lot of angst over a period of many months. If Matthew came to see me or even talked to me in the garden, it wasn't long before Elspeth appeared demanding to know what had been discussed. I was instructed by Elspeth not to discuss any subject relating to either alcohol or sex, as this wasn't a suitable conversation for someone of Matthew's age. She stressed that I had to be instructed about conversations with young people, as I wasn't a Mother. Matthew gave up university and was thoroughly depressed, overweight, listless and deathly pale.

The poor boy was not being allowed to actualise in life. Eventually due to the prohibitive restrictions enforced by Elspeth and my concern that this poor young man might take desperate action, I gave him a book to read, no doubt secretly under the bedclothes but I thought it summed up his situation and therefore might help.

I also gave him some back copies of Vogue and Bazaar with which he seemed really delighted. He said that Elspeth only read the Bible, church magazines and 'The Lady'.

Though he may have found a suitable escape route by way of 'The Lady' situations vacant classifieds.

The book was; An Analysis of Carl Rogers' Theory of Personality by Dagmar Pescitelli 1996 (with reference to Salvatore R. Maddi 1996)

What I was trying to get across to Matthew was Carl Rogers 'Actualising Tendency'.

Rogers (1959) maintains that the human 'organism' has an underlying 'actualizing tendency', which aims to develop all capacities in ways that maintain or enhance the organism and move it toward autonomy. This tendency is directional, constructive and present in all living things. The actualising tendency can be suppressed but can never be destroyed without the destruction of the organism. (Rogers, 1977).The concept of the actualising tendency is the only motive force in the theory. It encompasses all motivations; tension, need, or drive reductions; and creative as well as pleasure seeking tendencies (Rogers 1959). Only the organism as a whole has this tendency, parts of it (such as the self) do not.

Maddi (1996) describes it as 'biological pressure to fulfil the genetic blueprint'.

Each person thus has a fundamental mandate to fulfil his or her potential.

I could not have put this better and having had counselling myself have always found it invaluable. The Person Centred Counselling model by Carl Rogers is deeper than the Cognitive Behaviour Therapy that Elspeth sent Mathew to have but it is deeper, slower and takes a lot longer. Probably therefore not fast enough for Elspeth, as Matthews problem bothered her like having 'something nasty in the woodshed', alluding to some hidden or metaphorical horror like the novel 'Cold Comfort Farm' by Stella Gibbons 1932.

Mathew told me that he'd read the book and had found it really enlightening, so enlightening in fact that he was leaving home. My heart sank; Elspeth was going to kill me. He must have seen my pallor change to sickly pale because intuitively he laughed and reassured me that it wasn't just the book that had helped sever the apron strings and grow an adult backbone, but one of our neighbours. The truly lovely and kind Jane Beauman had been helping him discover his path too.

I was aghast as he told me about the dancing lessons he'd been having.

"Dancing?"

"I've always wanted to dance. Mum was even more upset though when I refused to eat anymore cake, I needed to lose some weight you see."

Not long after this discussion, I was visited quite forcibly, by a distraught Elspeth.

"You've been filling his head with ideas," she accused, "I know you have."

"He's gone, my baby boy has left what did I do to drive him away?" she shrieked, whilst blowing noisily into a hanky. I wondered how much time she'd got for the truthful answer. Instead, I said nothing and just listened.

Families, I was hardly on firm ground.

"He's gone to Benidorm in Spain to be in Cabaret! Charles is no help; he says that at nearly twenty years old he should be making his own decisions, for us as parents to support and not having us make them for him. He also said that I was making him ill. How could he say such a thing?"

Good old Charles, I thought, as sound judgement as ever, and I gave her a glass of wine and some chocolate, my cure all and assured her that all would be well.

"Charles is right. He is a big boy, after all."

Regretting this, "Grown up," I said, hurriedly.

"Anyway," I continued, "a different climate and surroundings should do him the world of good."

Blythe and Elvira stretched out further on the sofa, so Elspeth had to take the one and only fireside armchair. Elvira gave her a top to toe dismissive look like any stylish female would before dozing, looking very glossy in her own chocolate brown coat and new stylish Cath Kidson collar. She was known as that pretty little dog.

It was also said of Elvira that she was a gorgeous little temptress with a pom pom tail.

Anyway, neither dog showed any sign of moving or being hospitable and Elvira was using Blythe as a cushion.

Elspeth's drama unfolded, I listened, and they slept. And I thought how fortunate they were.

Sure enough, an email arrived a few weeks later with an attachment. It was a picture of Matthew in pink Lycra and spangles. He looked a treat. I printed it off and took it to show Jane.

CHAPTER 6

Jane Beauman

I first met Jane when she stopped me whilst I was walking Blythe & Elvira on the village green. I liked her immediately and so did the dogs. She had a laugh that was a throaty chuckle, the loveliest of smiles and the brightest blue eyes. A small woman, a little bit plump but it suited her. Pepper and salt chin length hair with a side parting and a little bit of a wave. She had heard that I was a decorator and asked if I'd call to see her. I took Blythe and Elvira home and I went over to Jane's house, which was to become the first of many visits. We sat under an abundant assortment of scented roses within her pergola on delightful old French wrought iron furniture, white paint, rust and verdigris.

She had a great sense of humour and a laugh that was more of a chuckle.

Jane's garden was an adventure. Little rooms appeared as if from nowhere and there were stone faces and statues watching where ever one wandered.

There was a huge rusted clock on the inner wall that had long since stopped above an antique Jali door that had a mirror behind and greenery around it that reflected the garden and gave the illusion of a secret room.

She had a little French hen house complete with

straw with a painted metal chicken at its door. There were plenty of hen houses around at the moment, but this was one of the prettiest I'd seen.

Jane sat casually making her roll up cigarettes and putting them one by one into her tobacco tin that had a picture of Tin Tin and Snowy the dog on the lid.

Roses were everywhere, in patio pots, trailing or shrubs that framed a lawned area that led to a summerhouse. Rose's were Jane's passion and favourite flower.

She made some excellent coffee and looked very relaxed smoking her roll up cigarettes and smiling.

There were no pretensions at Church Cottage. I agreed to do the decorating work she needed doing and we effortlessly came to an arrangement about price and payments.

It was always a pleasure working there and Jane and I became firm friends. I told her that decorating jobs were on occasions scarce and I thought it was because when I quoted for work it was as a decorator and not as a stylist, because although I offered all the things a stylist does, I wasn't qualified, as such.

"Well how about a history of art degree, darling, all the royals do it, it's so easy," Jane enthused.

So it was, with Jane's sensible enthusiasm and my research into suitable work related studies that I embarked on a three year foundation degree in Interior Design. It was hard, studying and working but with Jane's help, I not only achieved a degree but also some very good marks. And so it was that I became a decorator and stylist, which provided me with the sense of achievement that I'd always lacked.

Before marrying her late husband, Douglas, who worked for the Foreign Office and hence travelled abroad a lot with different postings, Jane had taught art to children with special needs. Wherever they were

The years passed and Hilda died after a long illness, the very same week that Cyril retired. His retirement was spent playing golf and cards with his friends. His life was ordered and quiet and he never had another dog.

So it was that after Cyril passed away whilst enjoying a day of golf and sunshine with friends on his favourite golf course by the sea, that a distant cousin thought that POD should know the truth about his paternity after the funeral. It was a relief to have what he had always suspected finally confirmed and of course, when the time came to leave I wasn't abandoning an orphan .The newfound siblings were really lovely people especially his two half sisters. He was so lucky but not so fortunate in another aspect as when Isobel's sister Nancy died she left her considerable fortune that she had made whilst playing the stock market very successfully during her lifetime to the legitimate children only. They all received one million pounds each.

I thought his exclusion understandable, as she'd never actually met him. It was on an evening almost thirteen years ago that I asked for a divorce. Totally shocked, he was so unaware that I was desperately unhappy and so very weary of maintaining such a monotonous, vapid marriage of servitude

"Unconditional love is what you promised me," he said, as he threw his dinner at the kitchen wall, unwashed tea cups hit the ceiling and their contents dribbled down across the patterns of stencilled grapes and vine, that had been a very 1980's thing to do.

"You make me sound like a spaniel; I just want my life back. We are getting a divorce and this time I mean it."

I remember feeling that I had to shout to make him hear, yet we stood but inches apart in the small room. The poor frightened dogs dashed away, afraid, they hid in the former marital bedroom. A sure bet, generally quiet, nothing much ever went on in there, they may have thought.

"I gave you unconditional love, but you've returned it packaged in deceit," he wailed.

"You go when you can no longer stay," I said, a line I remembered from a Martin Amis book.

Ugly words full of recriminations lacking in originality. Passionate beginnings to the middle years of mediocrity, a roller coaster of shredded emotions accumulating in an angry and worn down annoyance to the bitter end. Throw away words the equivalent of fast food. Instant, devoid of nourishment and full of bad things. Sometimes I used to fantasise about being his widow and how much simpler this would be than a divorce; he really did annoy me to such drastic lengths. I would wear a hat with a veil to hide my smile, be gracious for the whole day, and be secretly happy.

One day a neighbour gave me a bag of wild mushrooms that he'd picked. "I'm sure they're okay," he said, "but the risk is yours."

I made cream of mushroom soup but ate none myself, and waited but the mushrooms were not poisonous. 'Freddie from Elm St,' the horror movie came to mind.

"Do you know something," he said, very nastily. "I think you're going mad."

This made a change from being called frigid or lesbian. And so after much unpleasantness and distress, we separated and eventually I found Thrush Cottage, as it was then called. The words amicable, civilised and friendly are false if found in the same sentence as divorce. It is a miserable, dirty business.

Matrimony is a bargain, and somebody has to get the worst of the bargain.

(Helen Rowland)

living, Jane told me that she'd always helped out in special schools with needy children, wherever she could.

She told me some interesting stories of successes and failures with such clarity as if it were yesterday and Jane was now in her early eighties, though she looked younger.

She told me many stories about her life and the love of her life, Douglas.

How it was that Douglas asked her mother for her hand in marriage and how they had never, absolutely never had a cross word for each other in all their married life and rearing of two sons. I spent some very pleasant hours at Jane's both working and visiting. She was quite simply a delightful, kind and knowledgeable person blessed with a fantastic sense of gentle humour and generosity. She had so many stories that I always left Jane's company feeling calm and refreshed and certainly knowing more than when I'd arrived.

She also made delicious coffee from an old stovetop pot. The coffee was served in cups that she'd made herself.

Jane also swore by the health benefits of Jaffa Cakes. She maintained that not only were they good for you but they were positively slimming.

Her heath became a little frail and she had kept a mild but troublesome heart condition to herself for some months. She was of course getting on in years but she just didn't ever appear old. Jane was just wonderful Jane.

Since Douglas had died Jane had moved every couple of years, leaving a house a little more beautiful and certainly planted with roses, as she was wont to do wherever she had lived.

Jane's houses were lovely. She had shown me

photographs of the others and Church Cottage was no exception. One or two were in Hampshire, near to the sea. Jane loved the sea. One of her former houses was right on a quay, it was clapboard and painted black, but she missed having a garden too much and moved on.

Church Cottage was simply decorated with plain white walls, good antique furniture, exquisite soft furnishings and natural wood floors and doors. Family photographs were either in black wooden frames hung on the kitchen walls or in silver frames placed on one solitary corner table in the sitting room. No clutter but a few pieces of sculpture and paintings, mostly contemporary. It was a warm, calm house that was very welcoming.

The garden, by contrast was a mass of colour. As well as roses, peonies were a favourite as well as many types of clematis, encouraged to grow up any available tree trunk. Moreover, Jane was always Jane in her sort of casual land army girl appearance with the ever-present roll up.

She began to ask for help in the garden and the house and many a time I'd left, leaving her gently sleeping on the sofa, locking the door quietly behind me and posting the key onto the soft mat.

I'd leave lamps on so that she wouldn't wake up in the dark and there was usually a radio playing softly somewhere in the house.

Elspeth, strangely, seemed to be jealous of the time I was spending with Jane and on more than one occasion shouted across the High Street to me, asking if I was still offering cleaning services as if I was a working girl of the street.

On one occasion, I shouted back, "No just sex," and smiled sweetly.

Jane had decided to sell and move to London to be with her unmarried sister, Georgina who was a few years younger, fit and living in Chelsea.

I was busy helping to make the already presentable home even more so. I implored Jane to buy a man's jacket and some shoes from a charity shop to place in the hall so that they could be seen at viewings and then people wouldn't think she was alone, for her own safety.

She refused, saying that the worst thing that could happen to her already had, when Douglas died.

There was simply no answer to that. A few weeks prior to the cottage being put on the market Georgina had taken Jane on a little holiday and she'd had her bag stolen by some young men who had pretended to ask her for directions. I know this affected her badly. It wasn't the money, if they'd have asked she would have given it. It was the deceit and cunning that bothered her greatly. Today's world was becoming a faraway place to Jane's.

I took the photo's and email of Matthew's to show Jane and she smiled her sweet smile and said she was glad for him and that she hoped he would find a kind mentor to help him along in his new life, which was her lovely succinct way of saying she hoped he'd find a good lover. I made us some coffee and she said she was popping out in the car to buy groceries as Georgina was coming to stay for a few days. I offered to go for her but she said she needed a change of scene and that she was feeling quite well so I washed up the crocks , kissed her cheek and left.

It was just a normal day or so I thought. I went home and gave Blythe and Elvira a walk.

I never saw Jane again. It was early evening when Jane set off to do her shopping.

She drove to the nearest small town and went to the supermarket, one of those that have since been gobbled up by a bigger one. This particular store had one of those car parks with hidden corners, dark areas out of the way of CCTV cameras.

Like the store, it was due to be restored.

Jane walked quite slowly because of her heart condition and after paying at the till, she made her way to the car park.

It was there that a young woman with a large full trolley complete with a child in a seat deliberately ran her trolley into Jane and knocked her to the ground.

Jane was totally shocked and asked why she'd done such a thing and the woman replied, "Because you're so bloody slow and in my way."

She left her on the ground, threw her shopping in her car and drove away.

This assault was not picked up on CCTV and the woman couldn't be traced, though the checkout assistant did confirm that there was a woman with a child who was in the queue behind Jane that fitted the description.

Two days after the assault Jane died of a blood clot though it could not be proved that it was absolutely due to the assault.

Jane had driven home from the supermarket, had left the shopping in the car and went straight to bed leaving her back door open. She probably just didn't care anymore.

Fortunately, her sister Georgina arrived later that night. Jane told Georgina what had happened and Georgina took her to hospital and the police were called.

The following day Jane insisted on going home and she went to bed to rest and slept and slept. She took no food and Georgina had little choice but to let her rest.

ROTTEN ROW

The following morning Georgina took Jane a light breakfast in bed and found her dead.

She had a woodland burial in a bluebell wood in Dorset, near to where her eldest son and his family live. It was for family only and because Jane's house was cleared and sold quite quickly, it was almost as if she had never really existed.

When I think of her, I see roses in a sunny garden.

Her memory became nebulous, cloud like, indistinct I don't really even notice the cottage any more, it's rather like a theatre curtain closing at the end of a play.

There is a book by Mitch Albom called 'The Five People You Meet in Heaven' and having read this I do hope that the woman who assaulted Jane will one day face the consequences of her actions.

Beautiful Jane and her twinkling blue intelligent eyes full of life.

Oh, see my eyes
The sand flea cries
So beautiful, so blue
They make the sea seem dull
But then she hides
Beneath the wrack
She hears the tides wild cry
Give back that China blue I lent to you
As it sweeps blind hands
Of scrabbling suds
Across the sands

(Ted Hughes)

Strangely, I've never seen let alone met the new people that bought Jane's cottage.

Jane's house, Jane's time. The house died for me too no matter how beautiful it was.

Naturally, Charles, Elspeth, and everyone whose life she had touched missed her very much.

CHAPTER 7

Levi

I was impressed to learn that Charles sometimes held services for animals and he said to me that Elvira and Blythe were welcome in the church should I feel the need to pray or enjoy a quiet moment when passing after our walk. I think he'd heard about Levi dying, not so long after Jane.

I took a telephone call from my ex to say that our big old retriever, Levi was off his legs and ailing. I settled Blythe and Elvira on the sofa and with a heavy heart and a sinking stomach drove in an automatic haze to the former marital home. Levi dragged himself across the cobblestones of the drive to greet me. I got onto the ground with him and we sat together in the late afternoon light of a summer's day.

One of his huge lion size paws was on my lap. My tears fell onto his head as we waited for the vet to come. Simon, our vet, said the time had come to do the decent thing. I held Levi for the last time as he fell asleep his head and paws across my inadequate lap. My big beautiful boy. And so it was that I wanted to light a candle for my faithful friend.

I tried to visit the church one day, bearing in mind Charles's intuitive invitation and predictably the ladies of the flower guild were not in the least welcoming. In fact, I was met at the door and firmly discouraged. I think this would have been the situation with or without my little animals. My wellington-clad feet were viewed with the same contempt as Elvira & Blythe's paws, though all were quite clean or I would not have considered entering the church in the first place.

I have been to France, Italy and Greece many times and have wandered into churches, rich in their plainness and others resplendent in their gilded beauty and have sat or walked about and maybe lit a candle, never feeling anything but welcome.

Not so in Upton Greens Church. It's like visiting an overly tidy aunt.

Dear Charles does try to reclaim it from the clutches of the eternally beige brigade in his quietly determined way, but the thin pursed lips of the ladies resolutely continue to make their thick lipsticks bleed in disapproval, above the ample bosoms of some, shelved upon stiff folded arms and restrained bingo wings, to the hard angular boniness and crinkliness of their wrinkly stockinged sisters.

It is quite a beautiful church, typical of an English country village and for the past decade I have enjoyed my view of it, my walks around it and my occasional visits into the inside of it, taking in that distinctive smell that only old churches have, incense, coldness and dusty age.

CHAPTER 8

Black Bird Cottage

Elvira, Blythe and I moved into our new home during my favourite month, May, more than a decade ago.

Kahil Gibran said, 'Your House shall not be an anchor but a mast'

Thrush Cottage as it was known then was just that. A small ocean of calm.

Occasionally Levi was with us, when custody allowed. Levi, the last remaining ginger nut coloured Labrador Retriever of my former life, when I was married to 'The Prince of Darkness'.

Because Levi was old and his sight wasn't so good, I don't think he liked the change of house and preferred consolingly familiar surroundings.

So unpleasant was our separation and subsequent divorce that we had custody and visiting rights legally arranged for dear old Levi, so called because of his genes and pedigree being so exemplary. Ah, the witty pretensions of middle England.

I had an enthusiasm born of desperation to escape my former life and because of this and not wanting any more money going to solicitors and the threat of long court proceedings I settled for a fraction of what was my half of our equity and savings, stupidly forfeited my pension entitlement, as soon as I'd found Thrush Cottage.

With Elvira on the front seat and Blythe laying flat out on the back seat I drove our much treasured 1978 Acadiane Citroen van from one county to the next in pursuit of a home I could afford and in areas where finding some work was a possibility.

The criteria was simple, a small characterful place with a garden, not too far from a couple of shops and a reasonable commute to a nearby town or two.

With two dogs and occasionally a third, a rental property was hard to find, so the separation went on whilst we shared the same house. The atmosphere was as miserable as a really bad day at the crematorium, and I doubt there's ever a reasonably good day at the crem.

Elvira, Blythe and I lived in one room where some boxes were already packed. Elvira was usually on guard whilst Blythe slept under the duvet and dear old Levi remained neutral and ambled about the place in a blissful elderly haze.

I took one look at Thrush Cottage and regardless of the name, which led my train of thought instantly to pain, potions and pessaries and knew that was the one. In my price bracket, I had viewed a motley lot of properties. I had seen rats in alleys, alive and dead, kitchens in caves, literally! Vacant, lonely cold homes of the recently deceased and soulless boxes. I was also sick of condescending estate agents. At last, I had discovered just what I was looking for and proved that it was possible.

Sheds for sale at garden centres were beginning to look really inviting.

Thrush Cottage was as run down as me but I could afford it without a mortgage. It had been sitting around on the market for ages because although there were offers, lenders wouldn't lend on it without considerable works being completed first, or so they assumed. For example, the investigations of the cause of one or two prominent cracks.

I had once lived in a cottage with a crack that needed to be watered at the base for the crevice to close.

I had lived in old places most of my life and had renovated a delightful 17th century one in Hampshire, during a former life, so a few cracks and patches of damp were not that scary. Certainly not as scary as continuing to live in the marital home with 'The Prince of Darkness' and the rapidly rising legal bills.

I took a risk and I was proved right. Thrush Cottage did not need underpinning but just some repairs and love.

Consequently, I had Upton Green's bargain of the century! Having been lived in by a succession of elderly men, the last one now residing in a nursing home age ninety-eight, poor Thrush Cottage had not been maintained regularly, if at all over the years.

So using up what money I had left the necessary repairs were done. The outside was painted Farrow & Ball's Dead Salmon Pink with a gentle flat white paint finish for the woodwork. So many people use a hard blue tinted gloss white on old cottage's and it doesn't work. It's rather like old celebrities with new bleached white teeth.

The little fat front door was furnished with a verdigris ladies' head with a huge ring for knocking, an antique letter plate and a beautiful doorknob that I'd had for many years and had never had the right door to put it on.

I designed a Black Bird sign with the new name underneath to be made at the local forge. All things for a reason. An Albertine rose grew on a trellis around the front door and newly planted was a scented rose called Compassion, placed by one of the front windows where I hoped it would make it to just under my bedroom sill and a Rambling Rector rose to climb up and over the garage. I had bushes of rosemary with its little star shaped flowers and lavender in pots that stood in a row at the side of the little path to the front door.

Clusters of pots with herbs for cooking and decorative purposes.

Perfume all the way was what I was hoping for.

Contentment as I stood on my little old wooden steps in the sunshine weaving a trailing rose through the trellis.

Stand on the highest pavement of the stair
Lean on garden urn
Weave, weave the sunlight in your hair

(T.S. Eliot)

CHAPTER 9

Upton Green Village

The cottage had only a tiny garden at the front, about the size of a postage stamp and this was enclosed within a plain round topped wrought iron fence, (now painted in a flat white). Flat White. Blue White. Dead Flat Oil. Soft or Casein Distemper. Lime wash, to name but a few finishes. I am a decorator through and through. Like father like daughter, just a bit more upmarket these days. It wasn't so fashionable to be a decorator then.

There was no gate, just a gap with enough room to get an average sized car in and out, to and fro from the garage. Yes, bliss oh joy an actual garage.

In Upton Green's long Georgian High Street garage's and off street parking are rare and thus the possibility of obtaining parking tickets a high risk. For such a small place, it seems over the top to have such strict parking restrictions. Around the little village green are double yellow lines.

Thrush Cottage stands well back from a corner of the green and faces the church where there are a few parking spaces allocated for the requirements of the building, though there was always an overspill and parking for services was still a problem. The village layout is like a soup spoon with a long street and at the top the village green.

Hence, my Citroen Van was housed in a veritable palace with lots of room to spare.

The first thing I did was to install a gate to enclose our little garden and make it safe for Elvira and Blythe. I was broke but happy and literally worked to live.

Being frugal became an everyday challenge.

Never did a person eat so many jacket potatoes!

When the winter came keeping warm was a priority and I was so glad that I'd had a wood burning stove installed. One day, on a particularly damp and miserable afternoon and after several attempts to get it going with wood that I'd collected on our walks, (honestly, sometimes I felt like a turnip picking peasant woman from a Thomas Hardy novel), and with Elvira and a shivering Blythe wearing his scruffy red whippet dressing gown, sitting on the hearth rug practically pointing at the unlit fire, I gave up. I took the £10.00 note that had been given to me by a customer to buy treats for the dogs and went down to the local garage in the van and extravagantly bought two bags of logs and some kindling sticks. I gave Elvira and Blythe an I.O.U.

Just living was a struggle but I managed without the buffer of credit cards.

Not only did I collect firewood, I burned most of our rubbish, which was a good thing due to the council refuse collectors in this area being particularly choosy about what rubbish they take, sometimes I swear they did a forensic check of the bin, even tins have to be washed and their labels removed. I never objected to free papers and junk mail, all produced heat.

CHAPTER 10

Tokens of Lust

And then the gifts started to arrive, placed on my doorstep in plastic bags.

No prizes for presentation as they were all in Co-op store bags. No gift wrap, no note.

A mystery. First came the chocolates. I thought they were probably poisoned and put them in a box on a high shelf in the garage, too afraid to eat them, I was having a 'Midsummer' moment Then a bottle of white wine and I wondered if the cork was tampered with, so that followed the chocolates into the box in the garage.

I knew no one here and anyway I would have thought that a gift of a baked cake is more customary in small places. I started to look at people strangely and was so curious to know who my deliverer of gifts could be. Apart from saying a cheery hello to people whom I met when I was working on the cottage or garden or walking Elvira and Blythe there was no one that I knew of who would leave stuff on my doorstep without a card, a note or some form of communication and it was a bit late for a welcome to your new home cake.

A rather unctuous but colloquial new neighbour introduced himself to me one morning as I was unloading my van for the umpteenth time. He just stood in my way and grinned whilst the sun momentarily made his gold front tooth gleam as he simultaneously ran a mottled hand over a greasy comb over of black strands.

"Hello, I'm Reg Beasley, and I'm Upton Green's Chairman of The Parish Council."

"Thank goodness for that," I replied. At this comment, he looked vacant.

"Well if you weren't you'd be horribly overdressed," I said. He was wearing his elaborate chains of office.

But I doubt my doorstep deliveries were from Mr Beasley as I was most surprised to discover that he had a very pretty young country wife. Perhaps she was drugged or had suffered a bang on the head, and with six hearty cherubic children of assorted age and colour to maintain. The Beasley's have adopted two of their children, hence the mix of colour. The young Mrs Beasley was once more pregnant and I have to compliment the Beasleys for keeping the local school populated. However, it was a relief to discover that they lived in a large house at the other end of the village, as my preference is to hear bird song in the summer and not the shrieks of other people's delightful sproggs.

Kids being kids and having a good time. Earth Mother I am not as the maternal fairy passed me by carrying the biological clock, tick tock, tick tock; it's the no future clock.

The gifts continued to arrive. First red wine and then flowers, followed by a strange potted plant, which was actually an Angelica that was to grow and grow like the fairytale beanstalk every year in its dappled spot at the front of Black Bird Cottage. Its deep green foliage went well against the pink walls. As it transpired the Angelica out lived the bearer of the gifts. The plant more robust, well tended and loved. In fact, the plant was everything the man wasn't. Sadly he turned out to be quite simply otiose, of no practical purpose at all to a woman in the frame of mind of having left one desperate man behind and a wish to just get on with life.

Eventually the deliverer of gifts approached me. I was accosted in the Co-op by a man incandescent with disappointment and disbelief.

"How did you not know it was me?" he wailed.

He stood over me like a bird of prey mantles its victim. It was embarrassing and chilly; we were standing by the freezers.

Though I wasn't trembling because of the cold, I was angry, shocked and repelled.

I'd been subjected to priapic behaviour on occasion when I was much younger and now was much more adept at dealing with it. I was thinking of a sharp kick or a good slap, but was desperately trying to stay in control.

"How was I to know it was you?" I asked.

"Because you've smiled at me. You've encouraged me and aroused my affections," he said.

"I'm a smiley person, I smile at everyone, I can't help it," I replied.

"Tart!" was his reply and I was sprayed with saliva as he spat out the word that was a million miles from the truth. I was frantically looking around for some sensible help, none came.

"Well I can't help this either," he said, and lunged like a rampant Lothario. A full on the mouth sloppy kiss with a snake like tongue heading for my tonsils. I froze and dropped my basket of shopping.

When angry, count four; when very angry, swear.

(Mark Twain)

Mrs God Squad, Elspeth, just happened to be in the same isle. She saw me push him away, wiping my hand across my mouth.

I was furious and said, "What the hell do you think you're doing?"

He turned and ran.

It reminded me of a moment in time when I was very young and living in Richmond upon Thames. One day I was walking over the bridge across the Thames, laden with shopping, both hands full when an Asian teenager squeezed my breasts and calmly walked on, I froze with bewilderment and it had hurt, and here I was again.

The upturned basket and its contents were spread around the floor, as passive voyeurs walked slowly past, others stood still as if their batteries had run out.

Mrs God Squad, by the name of Elspeth was in hot pursuit, shouting "Nigel, Nigel come back, stop, it's alright."

"No it bloody isn't," I exclaimed, to the few bemused shoppers who were looking on.

These Christians do get it spectacularly wrong sometimes, no wonder they were fed to lions. I'd give one a passing snack or two at the moment.

"What about me, I've just been assaulted."

Elspeth returned, panting, red in the face, long unruly hair askew.

"He didn't mean it; he's having a bad day!"

"So am I now," I said, still hopping mad.

"You don't understand," Elspeth wheezed, "please don't report him to anyone."

I was just about to bellow security at the top of my voice. His saliva was still on my mouth.

"Has he escaped from anywhere not quite secure enough?" I asked.

"Not exactly," she said, "he's having a breakdown. His wife left him, taking their child. He lost his job, his house and he's living with his mother, who's very old and ill, and his sewing machine has broken!"

"What?"

"He sews," she said, as if I should know this and as if it explained everything.

"Oh, well that explains everything," I said nastily and then pleadingly, hoping that someone would understand.

I whimpered, "I only came in for some ice cream, I don't want to be a part of this madness. Is he safe?"

"Oh he's harmless, just a little confused," Elspeth earnestly assured me, whilst looking me up and down as if it was all my fault. "I'll speak to him," she said.

Elspeth was kind and generally well meaning but was also known to be as mad as a box of frogs, but I have to say the box always ended the right way up and it was a very grand box so they must be savvy somewhere, was my tattered logic.

Eventually Elspeth helped me to pick up my few items of shopping, smiling that cosy smile of the righteous as we made our way to the knitting pattern vision of the woman on the checkout. Never did anyone look so knitted. She smiled her vacant smile as other shoppers looked on warily at us.

Elspeth both in her attire and manner often looked a bit like the woman in the attic from Jane Eyre, quite, quite mad but busy, harassed and thoroughly eccentric, and I'd just been party to a scene of misguided passion in the frozen food isle. Most residents in Upton Green village resembled extras in a retirement advertisement for the over sixty's, minus the cheery smiles so a fracas in the Co-op was not appreciated.

It lowered the tone.

It was clear that I was going to be escorted home by Elspeth who was about to enjoy another opportunity to view my empty, materialistic world of wallpaper samples, storyboards, colour and paint. The lonely life of the childless divorce who has not even seen the light and has an unimportant job to boot. I was to be pitied.

The strange thing was that Elspeth did make me feel an inadequate failure.

I opened my front door; after all, it is my only exterior door, as I have no other. Elspeth as usual walked past me into my sitting room and sat down. Elvira and Blythe barely woofed, saw who it was and sat down resignedly on the sofa together.

"Enthusiasm born of desperation," she said and looked at me questioningly.

Elspeth as nosy as ever had glanced my message pad by the telephone.

Doodles and random words.

This was normal behaviour for Elspeth. If she went upstairs to the loo, she was gone for longer than was necessary and as Black Bird Cottage was so small it was impossible to get lost in.

I explained my doodling.

"Enthusiasm born of desperation is a little saying I have that equates to my life thus far quite well."

If only I'd prepared better for life.

"A tissue in the washing machine day is another."

"It was about a job, I've got a gap between decorating jobs so I applied for a part time evening position."

"What is it for? When's your interview?" she enquired, barely drawing breath.

"I've endured the interview already, last night."

Elspeth gave me her most sympathetic look, full of gleeful concern and waited for me to tell her all.

"Why don't I put the kettle on and gather up Nigel's gifts so that you can return them to him?"

I did both of these things whilst Elspeth followed expectantly on my heels. Elvira and Blythe looked on, impressed. She even did brilliantly at heel. I absent mindedly patted my van as I reached up to collect the unwanted gifts from a shelf and said, "And how are you my sweet? Are you having a nice restorative rest?"

I ignored Elspeth when she said, "You're anthropomorphic'!"

I didn't know what it meant until I looked it up after she'd left. Actually I'd rather have a one sided conversation with the van than have a patronising conversation with Elspeth at any time.

The dear old van is prettier and easier on the eye not to mention a whole lot more relaxing.

Infuriatingly she occasionally edits my choice of words for me, though I refuse to get a complex , I just get mad, and when I check the dictionary like the insecure person I am, I'm usually right, so then I get even madder with myself and my own stupid insecurities.

"The advertisement was for a food distributor, delivering food to pubs, so I thought I could do that easily," I said, hesitantly because I knew what was coming and it wasn't Christian charity,

Elspeth started to smirk.

"What sort of food gets delivered at night, poached salmon?" she laughed.

"Cockles & Muscles," I replied and with that, she burst into song.

Cockles and muscles
Alive alive-o
In Dublin's fair city where girls are so pretty
That's where I first met sweet Molly Malone
She wheels her wheelbarrow
Through streets that are narrow
Crying cockles and muscles
Alive alive-o!
Chorus
She was a fishmonger
And that is no wonder
So was her father and mother before
They wheeled their wheelbarrow
Crying cockles and muscles
Alive alive-o
Chorus
She died of a fever
And no one could save her
And that was the end of sweet Molly Malone
Her ghost wheels her barrow
Through streets that are narrow
Crying cockles and muscles
Alive alive-o

Elspeth was word perfect, and the good lady

laughed and laughed and the little dogs looked on.

"Did the job come with a hat?" she asked, and laughed some more.

I was thinking just how unchristian this was.

"A white hat and a white coat that I would have been required to work in but I was to store the produce here, in a freezer that I don't have, in my little cottage!. All I was looking for was a regular little job to top up my sometimes erratic income, and if that wasn't bad enough, the man, Reggie, said he'd train me himself and could we discuss terms over a gin and tonic and fish and chips! After all, we were both on our own weren't we? Then he patted my bottom and I asked him to leave.

"He was a slime ball, old enough to be my dad, and that's pretty old!

"Stop bloody laughing! What is going on around here? Is there something in the water? I've been assaulted and groped. Even the postman offered to take me for a drink because his wife has left him!"

"Um mm, oh, really, I didn't know that. Was there another man involved?" enquired Elspeth.

"I neither know, want to know or indeed care. I only want my post not the postman," I replied, not a little exasperated.

"Nigel and Reggie," she said.

"Yes a lunatic and a letch, but it's worse than that," I said.

"The postie," she said and smiled.

Elspeth looked on with the awe and wonderment of a child at Christmas.

A large and annoying child.

I was learning quite a lot about the mentality of village life, and suddenly I missed the anonymity of London living.

"There's the choir master, Cyril Roderick, otherwise known as 'Call Me Rodder's'. This really is very embarrassing. He fawns all over me, that is when he's not falling off pavements and tripping himself up as soon as he sets eyes on any part of my body. I only have to put a toe out of my front door and he's there. He makes a great fuss of Blythe and Elvira and I know for a fact he much prefers cats."

At this, Blythe and Elvira looked up in disbelief and Elvira raised one of her white eyebrows.

"It's like being stalked by Agatha Christie's Poirot!"

"Oh you're so right; he does look like Poirot, especially the shoes," she said.

"Yes," I agreed, "especially the shoes!"

"And the walk, a sort of waddle!" continued Elspeth. The demeanour, the clothes, the moustache but not alas his ghastly brash convertible garish car. He looks like Clyde without Bonnie."

"I know," I said, "he's just not fanciable. Oh, the relief of it, to get it off my chest. I've declined dinner invitations but only yesterday he said he had a proposition to put to me. I said that I really had to dash and did just that pretty sharpish."

Elspeth looked crestfallen. "So you don't know what the proposition was," she said.

She looked at me with pleading brown ditch coloured eyes and pouting lips.

"No and I don't want to. In my experience men generally have huge egos and whatever the proposition was I would have turned it down, therefore undoubtedly causing offense."

"All things considered it could have worked, you and Cyril. You could have done something about his shoes and the car. You really shouldn't be without a man to look after you, and at your age being choosey isn't an option," Elspeth went on, her head on one side looking pityingly at me.

I was experiencing a violent urge to slap her really hard.

"There must be some really desperate men in this village. It's like Dracula getting a waft of fresh blood."

At this comment, there appeared a look of disapproval on Elspeth's face. I'd once told her about the ghosts I'd seen in various houses I'd lived in and indeed I'd once encountered a vision outside in a suburban street and the person I was with saw exactly the same thing. And then there was my dear friend Carla who was physic, so tales from her were plentiful.

If that wasn't enough Elspeth once accused me of having an interest in witchcraft when she saw a Halloween picture on the front of some old local magazine I'd picked up.

It was snatched from my table and with a verbal outpouring of words such as disgraceful, shameful, serious, damaging, blasphemous and even etiolate. Thus with concern for my soul she left to go and track down the editor of the offending rag. She has yet to notice my Green Man placed near my front door but obscured by the climbing rose!

Elspeth often lapses unawares into that religious habit of belittling what is secretly feared, even about the most mundane things, small pleasures, and fun on that occasion. As I was obviously dammed, albeit temporarily, I decided I might as well have a bar of luscious chocolate and a huge glass of wine.

This visit was calling for sustenance of the same heavenly delights.

Elspeth often had the same affect upon me as the mood relaxing music usually played in garden centres; I generally experienced a strong yearning to thoroughly misbehave as the zombie like shoppers wandered around to whale song music, looking at tat.

"Sorry," I said, "but you must admit its odd this behaviour."

"I haven't told you about Barbour Bob yet, the Major, as some people call him, but he never was. He's been sending me little billet-doux. Usually notelets with pictures of Labradors with dead pheasants in their mouths. In one, he actually said how good it would be if we got together, only he was considering silver membership of a dating agency, and this would save him the expense! Can you believe the cheek of it? Silver membership too, not quite bronze and not gold either. Would that be average, I wonder."

Blythe and Elvira gave me a look enough to say, she's going on a bit, and I was, I needed to get things out into the open and Elspeth was a good a sounding board as any. This was food to her and I fed and fed.

Barbour Bob is quite simply a decrepit old wreck with a red and purple veined nose, but worse, much worse than that, he has creases down his revolting red or mustard trousers. He wears those checked shirts under the ubiquitous waxed jacket that are to be found at the back of Sunday supplements and is more plummy sounding than the old BBC. Also, how he actually talks drives me to distraction already. Words came from Barbour Bob in short rasping bursts, due to a life time of whisky and cigars, with intervals as though an internal pressure had to build up before they could be discharged in a splutter of saliva. Also, from what I hear he is intransigent in his views. Oh, and he shoots birds. As I'm a vegetarian and anti blood sports person, I can't imagine that we would even beg to differ. And then there's his nicotine stained handlebar moustache.

In fact, Barbour Bob is rather lizard like, an old

decrepit reptile in beige corduroy, checked shirts and waxed cotton.

He seems to lurk behind bushes quite a lot too.

A sort of embarrassing dad type person or a creepy uncle, you know, the type that bounces little girls on their knees for their own pleasure. I recall I had my very own; he was called Uncle Reg, Oh yuk!

"Anyway," I continued, "I told him I don't do dating, so I don't doubt he now thinks that I am either mad or a lesbian or both. I mean, how could I possibly resist his obnoxious, repulsive charms and his cheap offer?"

I've encountered so many licentious old gits over the years, in fact a whole cast of libertines of all ages, shapes and sizes. One day I shall write about them.

"Do you think that these annoying local bachelors are turning up on my doorstep because not only do I have a pulse, but I work and own my own little house, I'm sort of solvent in some work years and property, small though the latter may be and could be useful? Only I'm trying to be rational, it's not as if I'm in season and sending out rampant signals. I mean. Do I look desperate?"

Elspeth smiled her sly smile whilst I rambled indignantly on.

"You must see Elspeth, this is all getting a bit tiresome and my patience is wearing thin."

I was desperately trying to translate as eloquently as possible what was a load of angry expletives in my head, for the benefit of Elspeth and my reputation such as it was.

Ignoring this Elspeth took the risk of me screaming when she said, "Well it might be better than being on your own, divorced, vulnerable and without someone to look after you."

Through gritted teeth I hissed, "I am neither vulnerable nor so lonely that I am in need of a cretinous old wreck, desperate cockle sellers or rampant manic depressives and needy choir masters and further more why don't you wake up and smell the bloody roses, you speak like you're living in a Jane Austin novel! Now if you'd like to gather up Nigel's gifts I'd like you to leave. Oh and please inform Nigel that he can put each and every one of his lack lustre gifts where the sun don't shine. Actually I'd gladly stuff them there myself!"

I was to regret this comment, as not more than two years later, after moving to another county after his mother died and having even less success with work and relationships, he became ill and died suddenly. Elspeth said that he had died of a broken heart, but then, she would.

I didn't wish him harm I simply had no desire to know him at all, nor did I want any gifts or his tongue down my throat. Is that unreasonable, I wonder.

He was a man with problems. There are a lot of them about.

The choir master Cyril Roderick moved to another area not long after his unspoken proposition to me and this was fortuitous as he became rather bitter and took to strutting about like a very, very cross penguin

Mr Cockles & Muscles was never seen again.

Upton Green got a new postman who was just what a postman should be. Efficient and punctual, with a cheerful bonhomie.

.

CHAPTER 11

Barbour Bob & Babs Smythe

Barbour Bob latched on to Babs Smythe, a termagant little hag of a woman. In many ways, they deserved each other,

Babs was aggressive, authoritarian, bullying, despotic, dictatorial, domineering, exacting, oppressive, overbearing, peremptory, pushy and tyrannical and those were just her good points.

Barbour Bob would do anything for a free meal and they were as mean as each other. So he dusted her furbelows that were placed on windowsills with net curtains the customary one inch too short of the suburban house frau. He toiled in her neat, soulless garden at the steady pace of an ailing octogenarian and fetched her morning Daily Mail. He obeyed orders as well as any butler.

In return, he was allowed to latch on to her nipples and suck to his heart's content.

This really was what he liked to do.

Babs proudly announced this nauseating fact at a local garden party, early one evening when, very inebriated she was spilling more than she was actually drinking.

Babs being Babs later denied all knowledge of it. It was rather like the time she was mistaken for a black bin liner full of rubbish. She had simply slithered down the wall into a crumpled heap of an unlit shared entry to the cottages onto the ground whilst wearing a black dress. There can't be many people, past punk era who have been mistaken for a bin liner! Her unattractive teeth always stained red from copious amounts of wine and yellowed from roll ups, complimented her highly polished red talons in that they were both scary to look at, not that she was known for smiling. Well, after all it is said that the countryside is red in tooth and claw and in this aspect only, was she a true countrywoman.

She either walked with an arrogant strut or a drunken wobble and weave. It rather depended on the time of day, as did her obstreperousness.

Her frugality did not stretch to herself, for there were regular visits to a gym that had a hefty membership. A huge gold four wheel drive monstrosity, known locally as the pimp mobile or the hag transporter, so totally incongruous was it to its surroundings, and not forgetting her very gaudy diamante and sequinned trimmed clothes worn day and evening.

Her trappings though gaudy were obviously expensive so I was surprised to hear of more than one tradesperson complain about her lateness to pay or money left out being short. Babs was notorious for trying to get things for free. Neither was she a stranger to litigation. Her reputation followed her by way of a builder called Mr Derby, a huge tall man, big and honest in his dealings.

Mr Derby knew of Bab's from her former neighbourhood where he had carried out extensive works for her for an agreed price only to be refused payment unless he accepted a much lower figure after the work was completed. It went to court and Mr Derby won, but it shattered his faith in people a lot and he was a worldly man. He just said she was a poisonous tart and that you can take the girl out of the street but you can't take the street out of the girl.

Her late husband was a nice bloke really, for a bookie. He worked hard to get his chain of shops, so hard he dropped dead of a heart attack. He had debts though, that's probably why she downsized to a huge mock Tudor house in a town not far from here, but far enough from where everyone knew her and then downsized some more moving to the cottage here.

She's originally from the back streets of Bradford though, where she worked as a barmaid in a very rough dive, that's where she met Eric Smythe, her late husband. Her grown-up sons still live in Yorkshire, they've turned out okay, and both work at Asda and have families of their own. From what I hear, they don't ever visit their mother. I've heard they blame her for their dad's heart attack and all the debts. He made money and Babs spent it.

My sister still lives in Bradford and knows her boys. Eric must have kept my new address and that's how she found me, more's the pity. It's a small world.

Mr Derby's tale of Babs was known all over Upton Green and it was said that trades people would only go to her cottage if they were paid up front and in cash.

Bab's aged skin was as dry as paper from too much sun and she coated it in a heavy tan tinted powder, framed by hair with all the silkiness of a toilet brush, for it was bleached to an industrial strength peroxide blonde. A small feral person living in her own barbed subculture. An old groupie mentality kicks in, high on speed as soon as she sets eyes on anyone else's trades people.

Her regular drunken exploits like all of her misdemeanors, cruel comments and lies she has always vehemently denied. There is simply no changing her, it would be pointless to try, it is easier to accept her as she is and avoid her company like the plague. Babs is not good karma, she is a dark selfish cloud on a sunny day.

Attempting to reason with her is like talking to an evaporating cloud.

I have tolerated Elspeths pity and eccentricities over the years because of her very rare bits of clarity and her many generous acts, however it has to be said that she has always been unfailingly oblivious to the frustrations I have endured at her ridiculous verbal outpourings, some of them positively Mills & Boon. Unfailingly maladroit in most of her opinions and in her demeanour, Elspeth was also terribly clumsy and was usually wearing sticking plaster somewhere about her person.

Everyone in the village worried when she started to ride a bicycle. She stopped after a serious fall and bang on the head where upon it was hoped that the bang on the head might help but it didn't and for one who ridicules vanity she wouldn't leave the house until the bruising had gone.

On the other hand there was no good side to Babs she was simply vile. Elspeth is still doing the Christian thing of turning the other cheek.

I've never met anyone who manages to say the most inappropriate things at the wrong time as Elspeth, apart from my mother; it's a skill in itself. To a person who had not long to live I remember my mother saying. "Ah, well, not long now then."

There is only so much humourless nonsense that a person can tolerate and I've tried not letting Elspeth in but alas it never did work, her huge clown-like feet always made it to the inside of the door before I could close it. Village life is a concatenation, we are all linked by a series of things or events, fragments of lives, intertwined and choked like bindweed in Bab's case.

So it was that over the years, the true personality and misdemeanors of the horrid Babs Smythe did slither to light and they were very dark indeed.

ROTTEN ROW

Told by characters at random in discontinuous chapters that skip back and forth in time.

CHAPTER 12

Death of a Clematis

My first run in with Babs was when she nearly knocked me over leaving my friend's shop, Interior Theatre in the centre of Upton Green's High Street.

Poor Christo stood stock still, looking ashen pale and aghast with the deepest of dark red, almost black rose petals at his feet, the offending bouquet broken on the counter.

"Wow, what's going on?" I asked. "Who was that fearsome angry woman?"

Though I had a pretty good idea from all I'd heard on the local grapevine.

Ollie, Christo's partner appeared from the tearooms at the back of the shop and stated, "I heard shouting," he said, "whatever is going on?"

Christo replied, "It's that bloody woman again! Sometimes I wonder why I bother. What a thoroughly rotten old bag."

Christo was rarely rude or angry so this was exceptional.

Christo and Ollie are lovely people and run an oasis of style in an otherwise barren landscape of permitted beige, black or white on what is Upton Green's Georgian High Street, run by the Parish Council Mafia with Reg Beardsley at its archaic helm.

They can't be missed in their uniform of navy zip up fleece jackets, beige trousers or preferred pleated skirt for the wives, adventure sandals with socks and a shopping bag in the style of Roy Cropper. If only Upton Green was allowed to be more vibrant, rather like the individually painted houses to be found in London Mews or the village of Arlesford in Hampshire where all the houses are painted how they would have been in their period, deep and colourful. Arlesford also has watercress beds where the water is crystal clear. Upton Green doesn't even have a pond.

Still we're in the north of England and I'm told that it's meant to be rugged, not like the rolling gentle hills of Shropshire, as Charles the vicar, explained to me once, himself a Shropshire lad. However, the parish council has a Trumpton clock, a very small, blink and you'll miss it library stocked with nothing of interest but free coffee and biscuits every Thursday morning. It is the favourite Parish Mafia meeting place. We have a very small Co-op Store with a newsagents section for the purchase of the Daily Mail or Telegraph and one of those predictable and typical chemist shops that are to be found in every small place for the necessary Fibre Gel and haemorrhoid cream.

Upton Green has one Chinese restaurant with a takeaway facility by the name of Pinky Wongs.

Mr and Mrs Wong are incredibly smiley people with a young married daughter and her husband who have a gorgeous smiley baby. They all live happily above the restaurant. Then there is the Funnel and Gullet pub and guesthouse that is known for its pate and chips and the monthly Upton Green Wives lunches. Upton Green's husbands call themselves a fellowship and usually have brewery tours as a chosen day out.

Interior Theatre is a treasure for those of us not waiting to die, or to garden from dawn to dusk or play bridge or golf, quite simply it is a meeting place for people who like beautiful surroundings and have an interest in the outside world. There is the florist bit at the front of the double fronted shop with a selection of flowers and plants underneath an array of twinkling chandeliers. Mr Beardsley, chairman of the parish Mafia regularly bullies Christo about the flowers and baskets outside the shop and usually threatens him with letters of complaint to newspapers, yet the display is a joyous picture the likes of which would be viewed and accepted as the norm in France and Upton Green's new pavements are very wide. In the middle of the ground floor, there is a large area of interiors, furniture and soft furnishings, exquisite rooms styled and lit to perfection.

Personality, style, charm and wit as well as good food and drink, all under one roof.

At the very back of the long building is a conservatory within a walled garden where Ollie makes lovely food, cakes and drinks. In the garden, there are architectural antiques and garden statuary to view or buy.

A lot of their customers come from further afield, so it's a good place to meet new people. Generally, Interior Theatre is a happy place, even a visit from Reg Beardsley fails to dampen the good karma for long and I have never seen anyone angry in there or flying out of the door until the Babs Smythe incident.

You can take the girl out of the street but you can't take the street out of the girl.

So often, this quote was said of Babs.

It turned out that Barbour Bob had overheard a conversation about Baccara Roses being the absolute bee's knees should one wish to impress a lady. So without further ado and in for a penny in for a pound, you've got to spend some to make some investment mindset, he blew the three generations of cobwebs off his credit card and ordered a bouquet of Baccara

Roses to be sent to his new love interest Babs Smythe.

Babs thought that they were dead! Christo tried to explain that the Baccara rose is the deepest and darkest rose, not black but very dark red with dark bluing blotches. It blooms with velvety almost black buds that open to deep dark red blooms tinged with almost black and furthermore they were quite expensive.

Indeed, it was a generous gesture from her friend. The bouquet was delivered and left on the back door step as she wasn't at home and within minutes of her arrival home and discovery of the flowers, they were back in the shop in pieces at Christo's feet.

"You must have heard of Baccara roses," protested Christo, "it was only last week that you told me you were a trained florist!"

Having banged the poor roses on the counter with such force that she broke the stems and sent the petals flying all over the place mostly to land on Christo's feet she flounced out in a huff that Miss Piggy would be proud of in a waft of heavy Youth Dew perfume.

I asked again, "Who was that deranged woman? Was it who I think it is?"

"That hag is Babs Smythe, widow of this parish, newly moved in and already on the radar of Barbour Bob, old wreck and multiple divorcee," Christos said this through gritted teeth.

"Have we got any vodka on the premises, Ollie? I could do with a drink."

Ollie went off to mix Christo a restorative beverage of vodka in something healthy to counterbalance the alcohol whilst I helped Christo tidy up the petals. Vodka was usually kept on the premises for a restorative tipple after difficult brides to be, mothers of the brides to be, even worse and visits from any member of the church flower guild.

"Only last week she came in here telling me she was a trained florist and offering me advice and do you know what she told me a good tip was?"

I waited whilst Christo tried to compose himself. I thought a chant and some meditation was called for.

"She said that she saves any rose stems from the garden or cut roses and puts them in her decorative plant pots at the front of her house, so if anyone tries to nick , her words verbatim, her plants their hands would be shredded."

I winced at the thought of it.

It transpired that Bab's floristry training consisted of Floristry for Beginners, a day course run by someone called Vicky at her home, in the next village.

Another local resident had attended the same course and had reported to Christo how Babs had literally taken over the class and spoiled it for all concerned.

The Baccara incident didn't totally ruin Barbour Bobs chances with Babs as they went on to have a relationship of sorts but I doubt he was ever forgiven for bringing out the real woman in public. After this incident the real Babs appeared quite often, it was scary to some and hilarious to others.

She continued to go into Interior Theatre as if nothing untoward had ever passed and this is how life continued to be in Bab's world. She behaved a bit like a character from the EastEnders. One day you could really berate someone and behave embarrassingly badly but in the next day's script, you were friends again.

Some people were really distressed after an episode with Babs.

She appeared to have all the traits of a sociopath in that they are incapable of feeling much empathy and have little regard for the feelings of others. Guilt or remorse is a mystery to them. Sociopaths crave excitement because they get bored easily and are forever on the hunt for new thrills and conquests.

It is said that age does not offer any kind of immunity from the erotic interest of the sexual predatory traits of a determined and narcissistic sociopath. Watched long enough, a glimpse of a cruel streak and self-centredness is never far from the surface. It is easy to become drunk on their false praise and flattery until they have you firmly where they want you and they will always take far more than they give.

I didn't see much of her after that. I heard she gave drinks parties and was very loud in a yah, yah sort of way. Barbour Bob seemed happy enough and was seen leaving her house first thing in the morning, on occasions such as public holidays and birthdays. He toiled in her garden and was no stranger to a neat bush. He jet-washed everything, as instructed, that stood still long enough and from what I heard on the grapevine they had arrived at a most suitable arrangement. A close neighbour had heard grunts and groans of a sexual nature, slurpy suckling sounds, coming from an open upstairs window as he passed by on the pavement beneath one summer afternoon, and naturally, this being a village, he gleefully told everyone he met.

Now sleeps the crimson petal, now the white;
Nor waves the cypress in the palace walk;
Nor winks the gold fin in the porphyry font:
The firefly wakens: waken thou with me.
Now droops the milk-white peacock like a ghost,
And like a ghost she glimmers on to me.
Now lies the Earth all Danae to the stars,
And all thy heart lies open unto me.

Now slides the silent meteor on, and leaves
A shining furrow, as thy thoughts in me.
Now folds the lily all her sweetness up,
And slips into the bosom of the lake:
So fold thyself, my dearest, thou, and slip
Into my bosom and be lost in me.

Summer Night

(Lord Tennyson)

Babs hardly ever gave me the time of day and it is only now that I realize how fortuitous this was. Barbour Bob was decidedly cool when he saw me. It transpired that he had told Babs about asking me out so I was her love rival and not to be spoken to or invited to anything. Barbour Bob's early advances turned out to do me a favour, who'd have thought it?

However, we were at the same drinks party on one occasion and I was so shocked to hear them both talking about their golf club and the fact that there were three lesbian members. There's probably a pun there.

"Horrible isn't it?" said Barbour Bob, grimacing and folding his arms into himself and cradling his gin and tonic.

"Uck, it doesn't bear thinking about, men with men too and at the club! Standards! Things aren't what they used to be! And what about that low flying tart who's sleeping with the landlord at the Funnel and Gullet. Long blonde hair, industrial strength peroxide no doubt and skin the colour of a cheap brand of orange wood stain. Who does she think she is holding court like she does, in my corner? Hardly wears clothes you know, skirts up to her armpits, breasts in ones face."

This was said in the direction of a lady called Rosalind who just happened to be a friend of the low flying tart. They went to the same evening class to learn Spanish and it was Rosalind who first took Sharon, the low flying tart to the Funnel & Gullet where she was to meet Trevor the landlord. Rosalind was really pleased with this union as they were both single, having a good time and therefore hurting no one. However, adulterers and bigots were on Rosalind's hit list.

"So you're a homophobe are you? It sounds like you're an angry man to me, and by the way the low flying tart happens to a friend of mine."

His wet mouth twisted, no sound came out nor did a smile appear.

"She's a lovely person with a fabulous figure, or hadn't you noticed that? She and Trev are happy together and since she's been there, trade has improved. Sour grapes I think from a jealous old man. Besides from what I've heard you like breasts in your face and nipples in your mouth."

It is said that Barbour Bob went a bright red colour.

"I'll pass your comments on to Trev, I don't expect you'll be missed from your corner."

And with that, she moved on, as did other guests leaving Babs and Barbour Bob to stand on their own.

One day I saw Babs bashing the beautiful pink Clematis belonging to the end cottage with a broom. The huge shrub had been there for ages and was originally grown to cover an ugly electric transformer box, but this plant turned out to be extremely vigorous and obviously loved the place it was put as it grew from one building to the next to make an arch and was making its way down the side entry of the end terrace. People used to stop and admire it, it was quite something, and here was Babs continually pushing at the main stem and over the arch with her upturned broom.

I stopped to ask if there was a problem. The only thing I could think of was perhaps there might have been a trapped bird or something.

I stood there whilst she continued to bang the broom up and under the arch of the Clematis, petals falling to the ground. Eventually I asked again but louder this time in case she was deaf.

She turned and looked at me with an icy glare and said. "This is my right of way and I'm sick of this stupid messy thing touching my hair," and carried on with her act of vandalism.

Within a week or so the whole plant had gone. Lucy and Jeremy who live in the little cottage in between Babs and the end terrace told me that the Clematis had acquired Slime Flux as a result of the main stem being bashed and infection getting in. They said it literally became covered in slime and after taking advice from horticultural sources, it was decided that nothing could be done to save it. So Laney the owner of the end terrace cut it down and cried whilst she did so, the unsightly transformer box was in full view and everyone missed the Clematis, and there was sadness the day it was cut down, but Babs Smythe had had her spiteful way and her own industrial strength peroxide bleached hair continued to be horribly stiffly coiffed.

An old but prolific apple tree in her garden that had had many a gingham tablecloth spread at the base of its trunk, the shade it provided enjoyed by many over the years, met a sad end, as did others, during Bab's first summer of living in the largest part of the terrace. Her house was once three cottages, now transformed into one by the last owner.

The dear old tree's crime was that it not only produced apples but also those apples fell on the ground and had to be picked up. The damson trees also met the same end.

An Ode to Babs Smythe

I've a beautiful house in the country
In addition, my garden is now so very tidy
Well situated and convenient
For commuting to the city
There's an Aga stove in my kitchen
And Wellington boots in the hall
But I don't like to get them too muddy
For that would not do at all
I wear a Burberry Jacket
With an individual Leopard print trim
And fit in with the country scene
Oh, by the way I forgot to say that my Wellington
boots are green
With an individual Leopard print trim
And that my 4x4 is a fetching metallic gold.
I am really a country person at heart
And having lived in a town
I just love owning a place in the Shires
And inviting my best chums down.
My house keeping aim is perfection
So I have a char to polish so everything gleams
And I own every household appliance
Advertised in glitzy celebrity magazines.
Though my situation's idyllic
What a pity I never had warning
For how could I tell cows would smell
Or that cocks would crow in the morning.
I find the dawn chorus a nuisance
It wakes one so early I find

Though the church bells are tolerable on a Sunday
Practice night is one hell of a bind.
Already some matters are dealt with
The cows have been moved, who knows where
The cock was trussed up for the oven
And eaten, so there!
Now the next item on my agenda
Is the banning of ringing at night
My neighbours may feel disgruntled
But I'm positive I'm in the right.
Now I'm resident here in the country
Rural changes are long overdue
Though cattle look sweet in the meadows
Their habits are strictly non u.
Though I've made so many hygienic improvements
There is something not quite right, I fear.
Though nothing is said and at least by the vicar
I'm never cut dead
I don't feel that I'm popular here in Upton Green.

What was once a country garden could now have been an advertisement for a lawn treatment. There was a neat new stripy lawn, mowed to within an inch of its life surrounded by narrow borders with new plants so perfectly placed they were probably put in with a spirit level. Lichen and moss attached to old bits of the wall were thrown out with the bricks and stones. I had sat under the apple tree myself and remembered the garden being lovely, alive and rambling. Babs had ripped the soul out of it and now it had all of the charm of a starter home on a brand new estate. What had taken years to establish she had totally destroyed. Strangely, wind chimes were hung from every tree but not from branches that could be reached as she'd had all those cut off from her own trees that remained and also from the overhanging branches of neighbouring trees. The wind chimes hung from nails. Hence, they did not tinkle gently in the breeze but flapped as halyards into masts.

The synthetic looking lawn was mowed by Barbour Bob but cared for on a regular basis by a company called Green Fingers. A couple of elderly men who resembled Bill and Ben minus the large weed in between them, would turn up looking like the cast of the film Ghostbusters due to the large plastic canisters strapped to their backs to hold the liquid lawn treatments, with a sprinkler at the front.

Laney told me about Green Fingers because she'd met them on more than one occasion, not least their most memorable first visit. Apparently, they set to work on Declan and Laney's lawn as they couldn't work out the house numbers. This was a serious concern as they were dealing with chemicals, so Laney hastily shooed them on to their new customer Babs Smythe where they received a dressing down for their error and for being late and this was how it continued to be because they were always late, preferring not to work to a set time. Sometimes they brought some help with them by the name of Leroy James. What a dish of delightful eye candy he was. Young, lean, and fit with beautiful skin the colour of coffee. His hair was thick and curly and he had sultry brown eyes. All this detail I received in regular updates from Laney who was delighted at this turn of events. From Bill and Ben to Mr Gorgeous.

This testosterone fuelled young man for some reason made Babs angry, probably because he was light years away from being attainable so she was continually rude to him and barked her tiresome instructions. Knowing Babs, she probably had grotesque concupiscent thoughts about young Leroy and that's why she was so consistently horrid to him. Everyone liked Leroy; he was efficient at his work, sorted out Bill and Ben and had a great sense of humour. What's not to like?

He saw right through Babs and only wanted to be

left alone to do the job and leave.

They worked on the now perfect lawn and beds summer and winter. Babs had also employed them to clean pavers with a jet wash that were once an aged grey with lichen and moss to a brilliant white. So with everything looking sparkling and plastic Babs took Barbour Bob off for a two week cruise to the Costa Brava. Those two weeks were fantastic for the residents of Rotten Row, other neighbours and traders.

Rotten Row held an impromptu party and the couple from the tiny little post office came too. Bab's had given them and the local postie a hard time because she refused to be addressed as Rotten Row calling her house ironically Garden Cottage followed by the rest of the address. This caused plenty of confusion and a backlog of returned post. There were scenes a plenty in the miniscule post office but Bronwyn the postmistress refused to back down. Bronwyn was pedantic; no one messed with her post office or the post.

Bab's absence was thoroughly enjoyed but it wasn't until the end of the two weeks that something really hilarious occurred.

Laney rang me early one morning, the very day that Babs and Barbour Bob were due to return, she could hardly speak for laughing which was a delight to hear as only a week ago she had sat in my cottage and wept until her whole body was racked with sobs.

"You've got to come over right away," she said.

So I put some clothes on and raced over the road and down the village. I was met by Laney and Declan, her partner both had tears streaming down their faces from laughing. Declan was holding his aching ribs. I was pushed up the stairs and into their small back bedroom and there through the window I could see what all the hilarity was about.

"Get a camera, get a camera quick," I shouted.

This was going on the net and I thought I'd use it for a screen saver. Bliss oh joy.

I could barely stop laughing. Lucy and Jeremy were hanging out of their upstairs window next door grinning from ear to ear like a pair of naughty schoolchildren.

On Bab's perfect lawn now with two weeks growth was written in chemical weed killer, Yo! Bitch! Bye Bye!

What a sight.

On her return, Babs went ballistic. She banged on everyone's door asking if they knew anything or had seen anything, but as Laney said, she no longer pays any attention to the gates opening or being left open because Babs uses their back yard just like her own front door, and then there's all the tradespeople and deliveries from who knows what or where.

From a security point of view, it had been very stressful.

Not least trying to keep the cats from the road.

It turns out that Leroy James had gone home to the Caribbean and there was no point in threatening to sue Green Fingers because they knew nothing about it.

So Green Fingers set about repairing the lawn but not before photographs were taken of it and sent around for all to view.

CHAPTER 13

Rotten Row

"The narcissism of minor differences."

(Sigmund Freud)

To describe the phenomenon that is precisely communities with adjoining territories.

Many things were going on in Upton Green that I was oblivious to. Emotional under currents and feuds were many, not least in the long row of eclectic cottages in the High Street.

Not to be confused with Rotten Row the broad track running along the south side of Hyde Park to the Serpentine Road in London. That particular Rotten Row is maintained to the present day as a place to ride horses in the centre of London, though it is little used.

I can't say I've seen many, if any horses trotting along our Rotten Row either. These homes were in the shadow of Reg Beardsley's huge Georgian pile that took up quite a lot of the High Street due to his expansive garden. At one end of the terrace called Rotten Row was Jock Reynolds a linkman for a television channel. He was quite a jovial chap but he spent most of his time in London. His cottage was looked after by contract cleaners and gardeners and was more of a weekend place. Jock was a bit of a

Lothario, a legend in his own time with the women, there were always different ones brought back at weekends and all of them reportedly gorgeous. He had a terrific sense of humour so perhaps that was the attraction He once had a lovely wife, but even then, there were always other women but Jock and Ann seemed to have an arrangement that worked for them and they were very close.

Ann was a homebody whilst Jock was a gregarious social animal with all the carnal morals of an alley cat. In fact, he joked that he was a legend in his own time. Jock's saving grace was that he had a very kind heart and would help anyone out. He truly loved Ann and was loyal in his own way, although most definitely a wayward leopard hanging onto his spots!

Ann stayed in Upton Green whilst Jock worked in London, he returned home most weekends, that is until Ann died. They had three grown up sons, Ted, Hugo and Oscar, all as handsome as Jock. Sometimes they came to Upton Green for the occasional weekend and gave the local girls a run for their money. Well all except for the youngest, Oscar, who preferred his own sex and took after his mother in her artistic ways. He was a set designer for theatre.

The boys all loved their mother and used to spend lots of time at home with her, not least during the last two years of her life when she put up an admirable fight with her wretched illness to stay with her family and friends for as long as she could. It was a very sad day when she passed away. She died on a spring day, just as the daffodils came out, which turned out to be the last goal she had wanted to reach. Ann was always so much fun, industrious and kind. I have never met anyone who listened like she did, properly listened and remembered things in infinite detail with such clarity.

At the end of her garden, she had a workshop where she used to make wedding dresses, bridesmaid's dresses and beautiful wedding quilts made out of silk squares.

Jock used to joke that she didn't know how to sew any other fabric.

People used to pop in and sit on one of her comfy old armchairs to talk whilst she worked. Occasionally she had some help by the name of Esme Cleary. Esme was also known as Economy Chanel as she always looked gorgeous in her homemade copies. Esme was quiet and kept herself very much to herself. She got along very well with Ann because they shared the same interests and whilst Esme didn't have quite the same couture training as Ann, she was an excellent seamstress and would sew on beads and do intricate embroidery without complaint because Esme was happy in her work. However, she was a bit of an enigma, no one was allowed into her world, if the work hours turned into social, as they so often did, especially during long summer evenings, Esme would silently disappear.

She took Ann's death badly and Jock said she'd moved to Camden Town to live with an elderly aunt. Jock wasn't as good at keeping Esme's secret as Ann had been and told me her story not long after Ann's death when I'd met him out walking. He always made a great fuss of Elvira and Blythe. We sat on the base of a huge tree and talked about Ann and how much he and their boys missed her. I just asked what had happened to Esme, as no one had seen her since the funeral and he told me why she was so insular, so wary.

When Esme was about eighteen and living in Twickenham in a leafy road of respectable Victorian and Edwardian houses in a bedsit, she had been assaulted in a hideous way.

I asked what he meant by hideous and he said that her best friend, an Irish lad called Patrick had invited her upstairs to his bed sitting room for dinner. They were pals and she accepted the invitation gladly. The next day she woke on his sofa very late in the morning feeling ill.

Patrick told her that she'd passed out over dinner, probably because she wasn't looking after herself and he'd put her on the sofa, to sleep.

She apologised, her clothing was still all in place but she felt too poorly to move so slept on until she felt less groggy. All the while Patrick was concerned for her, asked if she wanted to call anyone, a doctor, perhaps?

She said no, and eventually went home to her own room and within a day or so was fine. There was however, something in the back of her mind that she couldn't quite reach. It was a strange feeling.

A few weeks later on a cold winter's day there was a plumbing problem, water was pouring from the top floor of the house where Patrick's room was so she fetched the landlord who lived in the basement, one Mr Usher no less, and together they went into Patrick's room, and there, centre stage, arranged in sequence on his table were photographs of Esme with a wine bottle stuck up her vagina and her hands placed on the bottle. The ring she always wore, a red garnet, as clear as clear. There were other pictures of her buttocks and breasts. They were obscene. Esme froze. Mr Usher just stared and stared at her and then at the photographs whilst the water from what turned out to be a burst pipe just ran and ran.

Mrs Usher was called for to look after Esme who had gone into shock.

Often the most fiendish of things happen to the most vulnerable of people and Esme was fragile in body and mind.

The doctor arrived at Mrs Usher's insistence, Esme was given a mild sedative, and when she was calmer, it became very clear to all concerned that she had been drugged by Patrick and that is when the photographs were taken.

She just couldn't believe that her so-called friend

Patrick could do such a vile thing to her. Mr and Mrs Usher threw Patrick out that very day. Esme wouldn't involve the police because she said she didn't want people to know. She destroyed the prints and Mr Usher smashed Patrick's camera to bits and had destroyed the film left in it, just in case Mrs Usher had also looked everywhere for other prints but found none. Esme had packed her belongings, pulled the garnet ring from her finger as if it was burning her flesh and walked away from all that was familiar, from her home, her college course in textiles and was never the same again.

Since then she has always lived like a beautiful little damaged mouse.

She never recovered from the betrayal. Ann and Jock's youngest son was at the same college as Esme and after Esme left, they kept in touch so when Ann needed to employ someone Esme was a natural choice and a little flat was found for her to rent over the newsagents in Upton Green.

Esme's pain didn't seem to lessen any in the cracks of time. She gave off an aura of fractured contemporary pessimism, skipping back and forth in discontinuous chapters, past and present. Fortunately, Ann had a startling degree of insight into obsessional and addictive behaviours and had spent many an hour at the local hospital with Esme after a session of self-harming. Sometimes she would know that something was wrong and call round to Esme's flat to check on her, usually under some silly pretext.

Esme would cut her arms, take excessive amounts of over the counter drugs, or drink until she passed out.

Ann was always supportive of Esme and used to say, "We earn a living by what we earn and live a life by what we give." Time was what Ann had for everyone and her workshop was a haven of peace. A framed piece of embroidery on her desk said, 'If words were money speaking to some people would be an unnecessary expense.'

I never saw Ann stressed not even when she had a deadline. Her commute to work was a stroll down her garden path through a beautiful garden. When Jock was in a strop once about having to be somewhere else, she said to him, "To be everywhere is to be nowhere." A phrase borrowed from a Roman philosopher called Seneca.

On hearing that I thought he was going to explode but a steely 'don't mess with me' look from Ann and he thought better of it and rushed up Ann's garden highway to his next important appointment in television land.

Ann's funeral was both lovely and heartbreaking. The local church and gardens were full of people.

Her eulogy was truly moving and in it was a quote from a child that Ann had heard on the radio.

'I plan to see the whole of the world before I die and perhaps the moon beneath my feet.'

And from Ann: 'Fortune favours the bold' a fortune cookie proverb. Humour to the very end.

When as in silks my Julia goes,
Then, then methinks, how sweetly flows
The liquefaction of her clothes!
Next, when I cast mine eyes and see
That brave vibration each way free'
O how that glittering taketh me!

(Robert Herrick)

The workshop has been dismantled now and a grand summerhouse put there in its place. I don't think Jock and the boys could bear to look at Ann's workshop, let alone go inside and see the tools of her trade, her inspiration boards, drawings and rails of antique dresses from where she took some of her ideas. Trinkets, tiaras, diamanté buckles, pearl pins, beads, feathers, silks in a myriad of colours, and weaves. A vintage dealer from London came and took it all away. Two years have passed since Ann's death and it's as if she was never there, just a lovely memory of a sunny day in a magical place of floating silk, muffled voices carried in the wind, laughter and bird song. Blurred edges to a hard present day, glaring, bright.

Ann's memory has become nebulous, cloudlike and indistinct.

Jock says that when he is in the garden he can still smell her perfume, Shalimar.

A small headstone remains at the side of the stream that runs at the bottom of all of the gardens, next to what was the entrance to Ann's old workshop. It is in memory of Ann's faithful friend, her dog, and says,

I loved you then
And I love you still
Beau, my adorable
And perfect boy.

Idealised through loss and absence, Beau was a dog with a sense of humour and Ann did tell me of a couple of things he did.

When they lived on Bishops Avenue in North London Ann used to take Beau with her shopping. They would have a walk in Kenwood first and dodging the mad tramp who had made his camp by one of the park gates, they would exit onto the main road and up and over the hill into Highgate village. Beau would sit outside and not move whilst Ann was inside the greengrocers and favourite deli. People knew him and made such a lovely fuss of him, he adored it.

His favourite place was called Best Friends the local pet shop that was down a little alleyway. Beau would have this shop firmly on their shopping route. One day on leaving this treasure trove of treats, Ann noticed some long rubber things hanging from Beau's mouth. They stopped and Beau refused to look up so Ann had to kneel down and pull this strange object from his soft mouth. He looked really indignant.

It turned out to be a black rubber spider with spiky legs. It squeaked and was now covered in saliva.

Ann and Beau returned to the shop spider in hand Ann apologised and asked if she could pay for the spider and the shop owner very frostily said, "Well it's not just the spider is it? What about all the biscuits and dog chocolates he's been shop lifting?"

Ann trying not to laugh offered to pay, "But how much she asked? From when exactly?"

Ann gave her twenty pounds and opened an account for him.

Beau had looked quite pleased about this.

Another time whilst walking along Parkland Walk in Highgate he took a Filofax from someone's hand who was just walking along the path and ran off with it and thought it was a great game being chased.

There were many many interesting times with him. He would help carry shopping from the car to the house; he had his own purse that he used to take out and a yellow knitted teddy wearing a red and blue knitted dress and hat. He would undress the teddy and bring the teddy and the clothes to be put on again and again. These stories of Beau were heart meltingly sweet and clearly, Beau had been Ann's truest companion. The loyalist of friends.

Apparently he never needed training and simply did what was expected of him, "And dogs do smile because he did a lot of smiling," said Ann.

Every year on the anniversary of his death, Ann would say the same thing in the Pet Obituaries column of 'The Times'.

In Memoriam.

A wonderful loving friend and companion. Months, now years have passed by and I still miss you so much.

Ann.

I like to think of them together again .

'Until one has loved an animal, a part of one's soul remains unawakened.'

(Anatole France)

All of the neighbours were supportive of Ann and Jock during Ann's illness. People sat with her, talked and held her hand. I'm glad Ann never met Babs Smythe and we were all thankful that Gina the Antique dealer didn't sell her cottage until after Ann's death. Everything just went on the same as ever. There was no disruption in Rotten Row at that time.

Babs had her eye on Jock who in turn avoided her whenever possible. He'd been snogged once by Babs when she was drunk and wandering about down the cottage entry. She was no stranger to a back passage. Anyway, Jock was keen not to repeat the experience and had had security lights fitted.

Next door to Jock were Jane & Freddie Harvey, they worked in the social sector and were absolutely lovely and so kind. Both worked with children with drug abuse and alcohol related problems so Babs wasn't too much of a problem for them, they simply smiled and got on with their lives. It was they who had mistaken Babs for a bin liner when she had fallen down drunk in the alleyway. They said she'd been looking for Jock, poor Jock and the dangerous back passageway. There's just never a dull moment in

Upton Green. Quite often neighbours don't so much call at one's door, but collapse on arrival at it.

So many locals smell of alcohol during the day, any old day.

Then there was Bab's three cottages now turned into one spacious home by the former owner Gina. Next door to Babs lived Lucy and Jeremy in the smallest cottage followed by quite a large end terrace lived in by Laney and Declan Delaney. At the end of the row was a right of way for Lucy, Jeremy, and Babs across the yard of the end terrace for trades people and getting the bins out for those two cottages and this had never been a problem, that is until Babs arrived.

"The narcissism of minor differences"

(Sigmund Freud)

To describe the phenomenon that is precisely communities with adjoining territories.

It had always been a treat to see Gina moving her antique stock about. Some things were put into her brick workshop to be distressed. We used to hear the slap of chains and hammers banging away and strangely, it was quite comforting.

The easement became a persistent problem for all concerned due to the antics of Babs.

The constant use of it, mobile phone calls shouted as she walked and the banging of gates or them left swinging open.

In fact, in the good old days of pre Babs all the residents said how great it would be just to knock through making one big house when they got older to have one long home sharing all the chores and paid help necessary to look after them.

In an ideal world, this was probably a good idea.

They joked that it wouldn't matter if any of them got confused and ended up in the wrong bedroom because they'd all be too decrepit to do anything naughty.

This has all changed and all the little slipways through into each other's gardens for parties and things have now been blocked up with any fast growing, preferably prickly shrub available.

Gone were the days of quiet strolls down the garden, at best they were infrequent.

The dynamics changed as soon as Babs moved in. She was a black cloud on a sunny day playing one person off on another. There were no more parties; in fact, there was hardly any communication until Damson Gate.

All the cottages in Rotten Row have long spacious gardens with views over fields where cattle graze, but the gardens could have reached the moon and there still would be no escape from the sound or sight of Babs Smythe.

Lucy and Jeremy didn't deserve despotic Babs, although there were amusing moments like when she came out from her white carpeted outside lavatory, drunk before lunch and announced to Barbour Bob "How good it felt to give the old haemorrhoids a thorough rub with a rough towel."

This was overheard by everyone as it was a sunny weekend morning, and terraces by the very nature of being a terrace are not lived in for their secluded privacy. It's down to residents to practice consideration and courtesy to others. For example, it's not courteous to have shouty conversations on a mobile phone outside the doors of one's neighbours and making their dogs frantic.

Or banging gates and bumping into wheelie bins and shouting abuse. The easement had become a noisy thoroughfare disturbing all concerned and the gardens were no longer the peaceful haven that they once were

.

CHAPTER 14

Damson Gate

Daphne had just finished at the library counter having checked out that week's collection of Mills and Boon and was returning to the library refreshment area, free on Thursdays, to have a little chat with her good friend Mary, when she saw Rosalind Folly. A name that conjures up a gentle woman wearing a tea dress or an author of children's books perhaps, that is unless you happen to actually know Rosalind. Bothering Rosalind when she doesn't want to be bothered is akin to prodding a wasp's nest with a stick.

She was a woman who didn't waste words, but did many helpful kind deeds.

"Oh Rosalind, just the person. I wonder would you please thank your lovely daughter and son in law for their generosity. So very very kind of them to let their neighbour Mrs Smythe have access to their charming garden and allow her to pick whatever she wants. Mary and I were particularly grateful for the damsons. It's a favourite of ours, damson jam."

Rosalind was beginning to look very cross.

"What are you talking about Daphne? Not Mrs Smythe or anyone else has permission to go into Lucy and Jeremy's garden, as you well know they grow their own fruit and vegetables and keep chickens for eggs to sell and use for themselves. They don't give it away! Were Lucy and Jeremy there? Did they say it was okay? I'd be very surprised if they had."

At this level of stern questioning Daphne was looking very troubled.

"No they were out, we were invited up to Mrs Smythes because she was in here last Thursday when the library kettle had broken and she said she would make coffee at her house as she'd just bought a new Gaggia machine and wanted to try it out. So Mary, I, Reg Beardsley, and Bob all went off together. Only Mary and I took up her offer of fruit from the garden though as Mr Beardsley said he had quite enough of his own and he wasn't giving his crop away because he had rather a lot of children to feed. Anyone would think that they weren't his responsibility the way he goes on."

Rosalind was looking really irritated as Daphne talked nervously on.

"Honestly Rosalind, she said it was okay and that she helped herself all the time. Actually she said that living in a row of cottages is just like a holiday camp, facilities all around to use and people to do things for you. For example she said she hadn't filled a single log basket since she'd moved in and that visiting trades people to the cottages had been most helpful at getting those necessary little jobs done and it hadn't cost her a single penny."

"Did she indeed," said Rosalind who was now looking very angry indeed.

As people go, Rosalind was as they say sound as a pound. Reliable, capable and utterly loyal to those she loves and likes but fearsome to anyone who she considers to be out of order. Rosalind possessed a keen sense of injustice; she liked people to play fair unlike her ex husband Johnnie who had played away more often than a top of the league football team.

Years ago they had lived in Twickenham in a large Edwardian House on Lebanon Park Road, near to the river Thames with lovely walks along the towpath and ideal for Johnnie's commuting on the main line from Richmond and then the city line to Bank

Johnnie had worked in the city and Rosalind had bought up their three girls, ran the home, joined committees and had her hobbies, motor boats and fast cars.

Then came the bad investments and all that went. It was a sad day when Rosalind's treasured 1958 Jaguar XK150 "S" Roadster was sold.

The two older girls stayed in their boarding schools and the family moved to Upton Green. Out of necessity, Rosalind grew their own produce. Lucy the youngest child was sent to a state school and Rosalind took a secretarial job and went to great lengths to make ends meet. Economy and budget former swear words became her mantra. She handmade the girl's clothes, bought second hand school uniforms and economised to the hilt with utilities, chopping her own firewood to keep the old AGA going and wood burning stoves.

Johnnie still went to the city and they managed to keep a very small flat in Knightsbridge by renting out one of the two bedrooms to another city worker called Jasper. One day Rosalind decided to surprise Johnnie and turned up out of the blue only to find him in bed with one of the cosmetic counter girls from Harrods. Her jacket with a badge on was hanging on the back of Rosalind's old nursing chair,

Rosalind froze with shock.

"You bastard," was all she said and walked over to Harrods and went down to the bar in the basement and got thoroughly drunk on brandy. It was in this state that Jasper, Johnnie's friend and flat mate found her; he'd been in the men's department buying new ties when he decided to call into the bar for a quick drink on his way home. Johnnie and Jasper used Harrods food hall as their local shop, which it was, though Johnnie should have been shopping at the local SPAR shop but he insisted on keeping his account at Harrods. Johnnie maintained that budget and economy were dirty words and hadn't he done enough by the sacrifices he'd already had to make? Selling the family home and living in a flat the size of a cupboard all week. Rosalind couldn't forgive Johnnie's betrayal, especially since she'd given up so much for him, the Twickenham house, the lifestyle and it was as much her money as his as she entered their marriage with a substantial family nest egg. Now most of it was gone and so was her Johnnie with Miss Open All Hours as the other woman was to be known forever by Rosalind and her girls. Though as the years passed it was said with humour and affection.

Not too long after their divorce, Johnnie married Miss Open All Hours.

"Too lazy to move on," said Rosalind.

Anyway, as Rosalind is also fond of saying, revenge is best served cold and the girls were sent to London to stay with their father during lengthy school holidays to maintain their cultural heritage throughout their formative years and were looked after by Miss Open All Hours who turned out to be as good as any nanny. Over the years they all got on quite well, it was impossible not to with the children. Johnnie and his new wife quite openly called Rosalind, The Mother. It was the way she said it! Harrods used to have a jewel of a bar, an absolute gem of a place. It was down some wooden stairs from the men's department and was everything a proper bar should be, polished wood and the atmosphere was mellow, the lighting a little subdued.

Rosalind hasn't been to Harrods since because she says that it's changed for the worst since that horrid little man took over. Everything Harrods used to stand for, style, service and tradition. Inside today, it could be any typical department store to be found anywhere, although it's probably tackier than most. But on that very sad day of the surprise visit, it was fortuitous that Rosalind was found by Jasper

Jasper telephoned Johnnie and together they carried Rosalind back to the flat and put her to bed. It was the last time that Johnnie was ever in a bedroom with Rosalind.

Being the survivor that she undoubtedly was, Rosalind got on with country life and bringing up the girls and as she was wont to say, "Our divorce was very amicable, we shared everything not least the house. I kept the new house and Johnnie kept the mortgage."

She had a sense of humour and she was kind. Rosalind actually went to stay with Johnnie and Miss Open All Hours, years later when Johnnie had two new knees done and helped with the recuperation. She joked that she only went to see him suffer!

She still wore her wedding ring and her engagement ring that was the size of a tasteful car headlamp. A beautiful antique that she never took off it was often encased in compost. Rosalind also was never without her Guerlain matt red lipstick, ever.

She probably slept in it.

Speaking of cars, she was a thoroughly competent driver who could manoeuvre her way around snow and ice never removing her cigarette from her mouth.

Rosalind was an unflappable, calm and confident driver. I've never known anyone drive or park like she does. Perfectly.

She once gave me a lift into the nearest town where the streets are frequented with sleeping policeman, we bounced gently over each one without changing down a gear, and the cigarette never moved.

She often said save nothing for best, everyday is

special. This was the mantra that Rosalind had been bought up with because her father was a survivor of Colditz and her mother had worked as a code breaker at Bletchley Park during the war.

Their home was in Surrey and when they became really infirm, the family home was sold and together they went to live in a residential home. When the house was sold to pay for the care home Rosalind inherited the family furniture with her brother Miles and Rosalind took on Oberon, Titania and Hermia, the latter being a very short and stocky little donkey. These three donkeys her parents had loved and treasured since finding them in an appalling condition. Their other dogs and cats, all of them rescued, from one sad situation or another had already gone to animal heaven having enjoyed some if not all of their all too short lives.

It was just as well that Rosalind had a paddock come orchard for them to live in alongside the chickens. Stables were built and they were content donkeys. They worked quite willingly one morning each year for as long as they lived for the vicar who really only required one donkey, but it was all three or none for Palm Sunday. So it was that Rosalind was reasonably content with her lot in life and her words were generally few, but wise

The exception to the rule was when she telephoned her daughters or visited Lucy and Jeremy to use their Skype facility.

It was whilst she was enjoying one of these verbal treats talking to her daughter in Australia that she heard a door bang followed by a lot of shouting. Jeremy was putting the kettle on when their back door flew open and a raging Babs appeared brandishing a green plastic colander. Lucy had been idly glancing at the local newspaper enjoying a quiet moment with Jeremy before going down the garden to clean out the hens, so the door banging made both of them jump.

It was a rampaging Babs, incandescent with pent

up anger.

She proceeded to bang the colander on their kitchen island, and before Jeremy and Lucy had time to react, though both were mute with fear and disbelief there was a truly shocking tirade of verbal abuse.

"Two fucking colanders full of fucking damsons was all my friends had. Two fucking colanders! What is the matter with you? You pair of stupid fucking hillbillies!"

Whilst this debacle was in full flow Rosalind had made her way quietly down the spiral staircase and made her entrance via the pantry into the drama being played out in the small kitchen.

Very calmly, Rosalind picked up the green plastic colander giving it a look of pure disdain and plonked it firmly onto Bab's heavily lacquered helmet coiffure.

Then she said, "Sit," and "Leave," when Babs made a move to remove the colander.

Babs obediently sat.

"You and I are going to have a little talk and you are not going to utter a word."

"I was going to pay you a visit so you've saved me the bother. I've heard all about your bountiful generosity and I am appalled. Firstly it is not done, simply not done, to enter a garden that does not belong to you when you have not been given permission to do so or to help yourself to anything in it. Nor is it appropriate to lead others to believe that you have been granted permission to take other people's produce. Secondly you must never walk into anyone else's home without knocking, it is very rude. Swearing at people is called verbal abuse. Swearing at me or my family is dangerous. Rotten Row is a row of terrace houses and the other occupants are your neighbours and not your servants. When you walk through the easement, you do just that, walk. You do not stand still, make ghastly unnecessary mobile telephone calls, or upset the dogs, ever. Everyone is absolutely tired of your antics and temper tantrums. Have I made myself clear? Your neighbours are all lovely people and there has never been any discord about anything until you moved in. You have shown yourself to be an objectionable and exasperating woman now go home and behave. Oh, and by the way you may be interested to learn that the two hillbillies here have an uncle by the name of Martin Hartridge."

Babs looked blank.

Rosalind smiled and said, "Let me enlighten you, the very same Martin Hartridge who owns the golf club that you and your paramour have been trying to become members of and owner of the gym that sadly you are already a Lycra clad user of. You can be sure I shall be passing your comments on."

Babs nodded; she was still wearing the colander as she was shown the door.

Rosalind said, "Someone should really sort out that woman!"

"It looks like you just did," said Lucy. "Thanks Mother. It's been pretty awful for all of us since she moved in. Probably a lot worse for Laney though, being the end terrace. You won't believe what she put poor Laney through."

Then Lucy reported on what is now known as Tree Gate to Rosalind.

"Only last Wednesday poor Laney was reduced to tears of utter frustration, she'd set about to work on clearing out her woodshed prior to an expected delivery of logs that very day when four fit young men with large choppers arrived."

Rosalind raised an eyebrow and Lucy continued as innocent as ever.

"Well, they went round to Bab's garden and Laney carried on working thinking that it must only be a small job they were about to do or surely she would have been informed. It turned out to be a huge job as Babs was having every overhanging tree limb in her garden removed, hers and neighbouring ones. Laney's yard was covered in tree branches, a bench and table were knocked over by the big branches being dragged past and then cut again prior to going through the narrow exit to the road. Rustic lanterns were left swinging. At one point, her wood for burning was on its way out to their lorry along with the door to the French hen house with Claude the cockerel who was having a holiday with Laney making one hell of a racket. Anyway, Laney went round to see Babs and you'll never guess what, she'd gone to have her nails painted, so Laney was left with all the mess on her yard whilst the first lorry went to get rid of the debris. She couldn't do the work she had intended to do and she'd got a screeching bird locked in the now camouflaged hen house and two distraught cats hiding under her bed, the noise of the chainsaws and the cockerel were just too much for them. Finally the gold hag transporter returned and Laney rushed out to see Babs and we heard it all, Mother."

Lucy was quite excited by the drama and was enjoying having Rosalind's full attention.

"What do you think you're playing at, you stupid inconsiderate woman? These are your trades' people; you should be here not me. You have an easement across my yard you do not own the yard. I only have to allow a walkway as wide as the exit and you've taken up the whole area. I've got leaves and branches halfway up my front door and back door, distressed animals. The whole place is chaos, God how I hate you, you selfish, selfish, inconsiderate bitch! Don't you ever do this to me again or I won't give permission for the workmen to enter, ever. Do you understand?

"We think Babs the bully must have been shocked at the usually reserved Laney's outburst because she didn't say anything, she just looked at her newly painted jewel encrusted nails. She is a nightmare and I'm glad Laney stood up to her on that occasion."

Rosalind went on to explain what she'd heard from Daphne and how she had sent word back to Babs never to repeat what she'd done and that she would be visiting to discuss the matter.

"So, every cloud and all that, she's saved me the bother, it's been quite an evening."

"Shall we have a little glass of your damson gin and another chat to your sister?"

"You go on up, Jeremy and I must clean out the hens as they're getting a bit smelly. We won't be long," and together they strolled down their garden, still a little shaken by the incident, but grateful that Rosalind had sorted things out.

What a woman.

Laney and Declan

Laney moved into the larger end terrace of Rotten Row about two years after I had arrived in Upton Green, therefore she missed the local lascivious Lotharios with their unwanted gifts and propositions, as by then the desperate of the parish had either latched on as in Barbour Bob's case to Babs Smythe's nipples, moved on as had 'Call me Rodders' or passed on, literally, like Nigel. All other derelict old wrecks seemed to realise their sad limits of attraction and left her be as she was decades younger than they were and certainly younger than me.

We had an instant rapport and spent many winter evenings sharing suppers next to a glowing wood burner in Black Bird cottage and some delightful afternoons and balmy evenings in Laney's garden at Rotten Row.

We talked openly and shared confidences as only women do.

Laney was actually named Magdalena after Bob Dylan's Romance in Durango released in the year of Laney's birth in nineteen seventy-six. Laney's parents were Bohemian and thoroughly socially unconventional people and this in turn had produced a very practical and ambitious child.

These character traits were fortuitous since when Laney was eighteen years old her parents decamped to Ibiza and became permanent residents and perpetual hippies, seldom returning home. There was no need as Laney handled the family finances well.

They had left her in charge of the family home where she rented out rooms to students and the basement as a self contained flat as well as living there herself.

She went on to study the history of art, obtained a reasonable degree and went to work for an auction house with an art gallery section, having an office tucked away in the eaves.

It was thought strange by her colleagues that someone so lovely, and she was very attractive in a willowy quiet sort of way, should thrive and enjoy her work so much tucked away in such a dusty old place. The dusty old place was however very ordered and well run.

She was always composed, contained and calm although she loved the excitement of the auctions and new exhibitions and bloomed with expectancy as opening days loomed, almost like a bride planning her wedding. Squirreling acquisitions was like a drug. Finally, when the exhibition came to an end it was like dismantling a Christmas tree and returning presents.

Speaking of weddings, Laney had been a bridesmaid so many times her friends joked that she was practically a professional one and could have been hired out on a fee-paying basis.

There had been relationships but all with the

exception of one had faded without drama.

She'd loved another woman once, almost passionately. Laney and Beth took long luxurious baths together delighting in self-indulgent afternoons of frivolous things. Playing dress up like a pair of silly girls and satisfying each other to the point of gentle exhaustion. For Beth it was a break from repetitive domesticity and the constant demands of her young children, for Laney it was fun, it was different, and she liked the fact that it was a secret.

These liaisons were clandestine. That is until one afternoon when Beth's husband had followed her and had listened and watched.

He'd seen them embrace at the door and had stood under windows getting angrier by the second whilst his huge manly ego and fragile masculinity were threatened.

He was an ordinary sort of man, Welsh and chapel. The drama that ensued was irreversibly damming and Laney never saw or heard from Beth again.

It was the end of a chapter, another one and Laney just carried on as normal.

She was relieved there were no recriminations such as an angry Welsh man turning up at the gallery.

Nothing absorbed Laney as much as her work and at home she doted on her two soppy, totally compliant Rag Doll cats Rags and Muffin, two little ragamuffin bundles of love. Her cottage was in need of updating but it didn't seem to bother her. Her garden was a long rambling delight, so she was content.

That is until one day as she was getting some groceries from the boot of her car and she saw Declan Kelly walking up to Rotten Row to the door of Jock's cottage.

All that was needed was a wet shirt and a lake, the

smouldering look and the Byronesque curls were all there.

Laney stood stock still, to this day she wonders if her mouth was hanging unattractively open, mesmerised and smitten at this modern day Mr Darcy.

The vision of smouldering attractiveness and dark head of curly unkempt fabulous hair disappeared through Jock's front door.

She realised that she was feeling that familiar excitement of sorcery and joy of obtaining a particular piece of art for an exhibition.

With great deliberation she knew exactly where this energy was heading, she was going to meet that stranger.

"Be careful what you wish for," said the demon on her shoulder. He was ignored.

Little did she know but Declan was asking Jock who the good-looking woman was that was going into the end cottage. Jock was amused.

Never mind eyeing up my neighbours what about my proposal for a glass extension.

I want something really contemporary and beautiful to maximise the light.

Declan was an architect and had known Jock for years as they both shared a love of rugby, meeting as guests in corporate boxes at fixtures over the years. They both shared a similar outlook on life and sport. Declan had a tendency to be more serious than Jock, bordering on the intense sometimes, and this level of intensity usually equalled his workload and he drank to compensate his stress levels in equal measure.

Declan was a true Gemini. He was two people a Jekyll and Hyde. Most of the time Mr Hyde was under control and not seen for ages, and then suddenly this ugly persona would return, resulting in the release of otherwise controlled feelings. The black moods had a forceful intensity. A force to be reckoned with, a tidal outpouring of all that was wrong with his world, the world in general, becoming stronger, irrational and totally unreasonable the more alcohol he drank. Drink was a friend to Mr Hyde. It was fuel to a sort of Tourette's syndrome, shocking, destructive, horrible, and very hard for the uninitiated to understand.

Dr Jekyll was charming, temperate, interesting, intelligent, generous, kind, and gorgeous in a moody melancholy kind of way. He was also very, very good at his job, obtaining prestigious awards along the way.

It was easy to fall under the spell of such a man.

Meeting the alter ego was totally shattering as Laney was to eventually discover.

She spied him through an upstairs window when he was in Jocks garden one time and felt stupidly excited but all the while kept missing him out on the street until one evening they both turned up at the same charity dinner. Declan was on a table with Jock and sitting next to him was a rather brittle blonde woman in a revealing iridescent dress. One of those women who obviously tried too hard. She'd seen her often with a plain girlfriend who wore milk bottle bottom glasses.

Declan and Laney looked at each other and that quite simply was it. A look that was full of mutual attraction and sexual charge. Frankly, it could have generated electricity. Jock picked up on it and smiled and alas so did the blonde who went into an overdrive of limpid, simpering adoration and hung onto Declan's every word or movement. If he'd left the table, she'd have clung onto his trouser leg.

All through dinner, Laney felt Declan watching her. She hadn't felt that good ever.

After coffee and speeches Laney, who was without

a partner and had gone to this local charity event alone, got up and said a cheery good night to all on her table. Then she walked confidently to the door turning and giving Declan a lovely come hither smile whilst turning on her heel to show what was a very good asset, her bottom, like a bitch on heat. Blythe and Elvira would have been proud!

Laney longed to stay, but she had a plan. Have a plan or plan to fail.

It was important to leave whilst she was ahead.

As soon as Laney had left, Declan turned to Jock and said. "You're having a party next weekend, I'll pay for everything, just make sure that neighbour of yours can come."

Jock laughed straight from the belly, the blonde who had overheard slithered over to her own seat.

Declan could hardly wait. Jock rang Laney the following day and said he was having a party next Saturday and would she come?

"I'd love to. Should I bring a partner?"

"God no," exclaimed Jock, before gathering his wits. "Er, um, do you have a boyfriend?"

"No I don't," replied Laney smiling.

"Just you then lovely girl, just you."

"Eight o'clock no need to bring anything, just yourself, bye now."

"Bloody exhausting this subterfuge, but she hasn't got a man in her life, so the parties on," is what Jock said to Declan as soon as he'd spoken to Laney and then began ordering wine and booking the caterers. Jock was an old romantic, he set about hanging fairy lights in the branches of the bare wintery trees and hung Ann's bunting between them so she would be a part of everything still.

Everything in hand he left for work in London, wondering whom he should invite to be his partner for the party.

His diary read like a typical man about town. He had women friends for all sorts of occasions.

That evening he rang around friends and neighbours and all accepted. Winter guest acceptance is always more successful without the summer holidays when people are away.

There were a few people that he deliberately missed off the guest list such as the woman whom Declan had taken to the charity dinner, Sharon, and her gossiping harpies.

A local crowd of Stepford Wives minus their husbands, who would attend the opening of an envelope if wine were on offer. They were known for turning up to parties with the cheapest bottles of plonk available at Aldi or Lidl and then taking good bottles from the table and hiding them beneath their chairs to drink themselves. Or in a sharing situation whilst sitting at a table, they would fill their glasses to the brim and bend down to the glass to slurp.

It was hard to invite these four women to anything, as they were never singular, always a group. Their forte was moaning about men and drinking, smoking, avoiding work and having a good time. Their pursuit of pleasure and intoxicated oblivion was a full time activity for this small coven. Sharon was an elderly Barbie with brittle bones, a sharp tongue and a wizened face. Penny had those milk bottle bottom glasses and the haircut of a period drama half-wit. Steph was clinging on desperately to the seventies. She was probably the best of the four. On her own, she was really quite nice but the others seldom allowed her to be.

Patchouli oils and josh sticks, pale pink pearly

lipstick, long bleached blonde hair with a shaggy fringe and hippy clothes or jeans and flowing white shirt and long, long boots. From the back, she could have passed for a young girl but it was a shocking disappointment when viewed from the front because although only in her thirties her complexion was a mesh of broken veins, her eyes glistened and were red and glazed with the effects of drink.

But in Steph's head, she was as beautiful, and why not because if you took away the addictions she was? Steph was vulnerable and easily led.

Then there was Debs, dirty Debs, as she was known. Debs always looked like she needed a bath and a good scrub, often wrapped around a wine bottle and openly taking drugs.

These four Upton Green thirty something mothers, all married, in Sharon's case three times, were inseparable, seldom apart, only one of them worked, and that was Steph who worked in a wine shop on Saturdays, probably for the staff discounts. Steph also had a regular lover. Quite a few women of assorted ages shared this particular lover and none seemed to mind.

He was a big amenable tomcat. His name was Jag and he was a short cherubic man with a scary physic of oiled and tattooed muscles. His everyday attire regardless of the season was cropped jersey jogging bottoms, a vest and trainers and with more ironware on chains, his ears or other piercings than a scrap merchant. He was surprisingly and uproariously funny and kind and he made some beautiful babies. There were several about the place and each one gorgeous, beautific and smiley easy babies. He was often seen sitting outside the Funnel and Gullet bouncing a baby on his knee. Then and only then did he abstain from alcohol. He'd flit about in an old red Porsche. No one knew how he made his money, but there were always wads of notes in the pockets of the jersey cropped jogging bottoms. Sometimes he would help out with the watering of Upton Green's hanging baskets and this was a truly incongruous sight to behold. He would pull the wheeled water tank effortlessly whilst smoking a roll up and sit on the pavement, hose in hand, a direct hit on the baskets and scary for old ladies. The girly afternoons of Steph, Sharon, Debs and Penny were spent drinking and smoking in each other's kitchens and moaning about the unfairness of life whilst comparing their fake tans and manicures.

Their children, depending on whose kitchen the coven were meeting in that day would arrive home to a smog of cigarette smoke and the toxic tired smell of booze.

They were all really nice responsible kids.

The women seemed to live in their own narrow little worlds somewhere between the local pub and wine shop. Maybe they weren't so stupid after all.

The problem was that if you offended one of them you offended them all and Laney had certainly upset Sharon by just being on the planet and being noticed by Jock. Consequently, Jock was worried and was going to try to keep the party a bit of a secret as the four harpies never let the lack of an invitation bother them and turned up anyway.

Babs and Barbour Bob were not invited for obvious reasons; folk didn't want to be in the same room as Babs.

Her reputation wobbled before her.

Recently Barbour Bob had been invited to a country society wedding by way of an old associate and naturally, he took Babs as his guest.

Apparently, she got very inebriated and the vicar who was also a guest could tolerate no more when she tried to dance the gay Gordons and divulged to everyone a Germaline pink gussetless corset and suspenders. The best man who had been dragged on the floor to dance with her announced he was thinking of turning gay and was last seen heading for the hills looking for a Broke Back Mountain situation.

Christo and Olly who were guests at the wedding as well being the florists realised once more how wonderful it was to have each other.

As they watched transfixed as Babs was forcibly led from the room. Both looked on with distaste at the acid yellow and black dress and jacket suit with a matching fascinator that Babs was wearing. They were still feeling queasy about the clashing spandex gussetless underwear when Christo had a most reassuring thought.

It was that this shameful spectacle made his own entry all those years ago into a juvenile punk band, having dyed his hair electric blue with shocking pink tips and wearing his mother's angora cerise pink bed jacket with bondage trousers, was after all retrospectively tasteful. Christo had a faultless reputation for impeccable taste these days and worried that his pretty punk era would turn up on Facebook, but at least he never looked as bad as vile old Babs.

Elspeth was also enjoying Barbour Bob's disgrace at his partner's atrocious behaviour.

She was loving it as the sympathetic smile was obviously turning into a smirk, she could hardly wait to tell everyone about it in the guise of concerned vicar's wife.

She would be brazen enough to call on Babs too. In fact, she did the very next day and was told to clear off, bloody do gooder. Elspeth just smiled that infuriating, condescending smile of hers and said, "Oh dear, I'll call again when you're feeling better."

She was her usual impervious self.

As was usual Babs went on as if nothing had happened and was angry with the vicar for ruining her evening.

The party preparations were going well, everything was organised.

Jock was really looking forward to seeing Declan and Laney together and being able to watch the obvious attraction unfold. It was worth putting on a party for he thought but anyway he loved a good party and his were always good.

Saturday was a bright winter's day and dry so far. The wine arrived, and late that afternoon the caterers came to prepare and lay out the food.

Jock's sons, Ted, Hugo and Oscar were there so they were in charge of music, setting up, and manning the bar. They also had their guitars at the ready.

They were amused that Declan was on tender hooks and was nervously pacing the floor.

He had quizzed Jock so many times about what Laney had actually said on accepting the party invitation.

"What if she's ill? Have you seen her this week? What if I imagined this amazing attraction?"

"Actually I saw her this morning walking over to see her friend at Black Bird Cottage and she looked just as beautiful as last week," reported Jock.

"Friend? What friend?" asked Declan.

"A lovely woman by the name of Louisa Dearly. Ann had lots of time for Louisa. I haven't seen much of her lately, she's got a big decorating job on and she stays there quite a lot apparently. Well at least that's what she says she's doing." said Jack and laughed, because he'd seen Louisa arrive via his back door with the church candles he'd asked her to collect for him. She had smiled and left before anyone else had seen her, except for the caterers.

"Decorating job?" asked Declan, quizzically.

"Yes, she's a decorator stylist type person."

"Oh," replied Declan, relieved that the friend was female.

Already jealousy was in its infancy rearing its ugly little head.

Jock lit a fire in the inglenook and lit big church candles in storm lanterns. The outside lights were switched on and the fairy lights twinkled in the trees. Ann's silk bunting of jewel colours fluttered in the breeze. Ted, Hugo and Oscar messed about on the guitars and Jock toasted teacakes and crumpets and made a big pot of tea.

With melting butter and thick fruity jam. It was a cosy banquet as five hungry males tucked in.

Jock joked with Declan that his appetite was still okay.

The scene was set with three hours to go before the party started.

I knew all about Jock's friend from Laney and could hardly wait to meet Declan Kelly. Laney and I had decided to arrive at the party together.

Laney was both nervous and excited, and was having the same worries as Declan. "What if I imagined the mutual attraction? It could be like that dress you've just got to have until you get it and then not really like it."

"Well you've got nothing to lose, just enjoy the party. Relax, be yourself," I said.

Blythe and Elvira were concentrating on Laney, convinced that they could smell cat and were on full alert.

"I won't be staying late because I'm working tomorrow," I said.

"This is a big job isn't it? You're never at home these days. How's it going?" asked Laney.

"Oh really good but I need to be there all the time, you know how it is with suppliers and contractors."

Elvira raised one grey eyebrow in the style of Joan Crawford and the subject was changed to what to wear for the party.

Laney had bought an indigo blue ankle length velvet dress that was perfectly simple, sexy and warm as she couldn't bear being cold. She intended wearing little suede ankle boots and some delicate antique jewellery.

My choice was to be a little pink short dress and a favourite black jacket with fabric vintage over the knee boots. I was in a pink frame of mind.

Laney admired my freshly painted kitchen and had a good laugh at my rebellious artwork.

I walked Elvira and Blythe, made a few calls and cuddled on the sofa with my two contented dogs whilst watching a Bette Davies film, 'All about Eve'. Well that's what I tried to do but alas, as soon as Elspeth saw the lights on and smoke from the chimney she came bounding up to my door like a Greyhound released from a trap.

Blythe groaned like any man would do when I moved him. He'd just got really comfortable when a warm lap was removed from under a sleepy head.

Elvira got off the sofa, grabbed one her soft toys around the throat and could be heard padding up the stairs.

Elspeth's large feet encased in boat like Mary Janes entered the small sitting room first. With two large strides, she had seated herself down and was speed reading the upside down mail on an occasional table.

The interrogation began. "Where have you been? You haven't answered my calls. Have you found a boyfriend yet? You have, I can tell. Who is it?"

"I'm working Elspeth. I wish you'd stop inferring that I'm desperate for a man."

"You're so elusive; he's not married is he?" she said.

The multiple questioning was ignored.

"Hello Elspeth. How are you?"

"Well, I'm very well and as busy as ever what with my charity work and visiting the sick and needy."

"Same old, same old then," I muttered, and before she could say anything I quickly continued, "how's Matthew, have you heard from him lately?"

"I've pleaded for him to come home. I've told him we can sort this out and he can have more counselling and now he doesn't return my calls or emails."

"Perhaps you should have counselling to come to terms with your son's sexuality, Elspeth."

"I wouldn't expect you to understand, it's not as if you're a mother."

Blythe and Elvira begged to differ but just growled softly.

"Anyway you haven't answered any of my questions."

"Probably because you keep asking the same ones over and over. I've already told you Elspeth I have a really big decorating job on so I stay over as there is accommodation available to me. It is a very large house undergoing an extensive refurbishment and I need to be on site. Would you like some coffee Elspeth?"

"Thank you, yes."

As ever Elspeth followed me into the kitchen.

"Good heavens, what have you done?"

"Oh, I did this last night, don't you like it?"

"Everywhere is pink!"

"Yes I quite fancied a pink kitchen."

The walls and ceiling were painted matt pale pink, the tongue and groove cupboards cerise. The small kitchen window had a cerise blind and curtains with a white background and a repeat pattern of baby blue, pink and grey edged teacups, saucers and plates. The crockery on the shelves above the cerise cupboards was assorted patterns of blue Burleigh. On the only remaining wall, space floor to ceiling was graffiti art freshly done on a pink canvas with large sprawling black letters.

It said:

YESTERDAY I WAS BLUE

TODAY I AM PINK

IN A ROSY GLOW

I MAY BE SMART

OR JUST A LOVELY TART

BUT KEEP BUYING THE CRAP

OR WE'LL ALL BE FUCKED

LAND FILL IS GOOD

DON'T SHOW THIS TO YOUR MOTHER.

HA HA

The black paint had run, effectively.

"Did you do this, Louisa?"

"Who else? Of course I did it's my kitchen and its fun I love it, it's only paint and a few graphics."

"It's disgraceful and I'm really worried about you. You'll never find a man. You are not seriously leaving that on the wall. It's obscene."

"It's not. I like it. And landfill can be good. I saw a wildlife programme on it only last week and did you know that energy can be generated from waste and when the site is full it is turned back to nature and it's a great habitat for wildlife. Mind you I keep getting this picture in my head of some little creature burrowing and banging it's head on old prams and stuff."

"Not that, Louisa, that's not what I mean," said Elspeth, looking disgusted and incredulous. "You've got the 'f' word on your wall."

"Well the 'c' word wasn't contextual. I could use that for upstairs though."

"Stop being facetious, Louisa."

"It's a deal Elspeth. If you stop engaging in an archaic chagrin attitude. Lighten up."

The kettle's little bird, also pink started to whistle. Saved by the bell.

"Biscuits? Shop bought, of course?"

The tray was loaded and we went back into the sitting room.

"So what's this house like then? Whom are you working for? You usually have samples and stuff around."

"Storyboards you mean? Everything is there in situ

so I've no need to bring stuff home, which is really good, as I don't exactly have much room here. Anyway, I don't want to talk about it until it's finished. It's sort of evolving if you know what I mean. It's very exciting though. I'm loving every minute of it and Blythe and Elvira are enjoying a change of scene. We're not missing death row or the cowpats. I'm not reminded of my own mortality several times a day. I feel free, younger even."

Elspeth huffed uncharitably as was her way.

"Are you sure you haven't got one of those live in jobs from The Lady? You can tell me. After all being in service and living in is nothing to be ashamed of, someone has to do it. Is this your day off?"

"Aristotle was right wasn't he Elspeth, when he said that we are what we repeatedly do. Because you sure as hell are a patronising pain in the arse time and time again."

"I only asked a question. There's no need to be offensive," said Elspeth.

"Oh it's all right for you to belittle my work to the point of believing it doesn't exist. Christ Elspeth, are you aware of how insulting that is to me?"

"Don't be sacrilegious; there is no need to bring Christ into this!"

"Oh God, Elspeth, you are unbelievable."

"You are thoroughly wicked, Louisa!"

"Oh cool, to quote Mathew."

"Don't you bring my poor mislead son into this. I'm leaving!"

"So soon?"

And the door slammed shut.

Two seconds later she returned as she'd forgotten her purse.

"What's going on across the green at Jock's cottage?" she asked, the discord of only moments ago gone.

"A party," I answered, as we both watched as the caterers unloaded their van.

"Showbiz folk I expect," said Elspeth. "I don't suppose you've had an invite either?"

"Actually I have. I'm going with Laney as an actual guest, not to do the bar, waitress or clean, amazing isn't it?"

"Two single women of the parish together," said Elspeth rubbing her large chin.

"Well, it's obvious it must be a singles party that's why you haven't had an invite. I can't think of any other reason can you Elspeth?"

Then a wine merchants van arrived and its contents tinkled as they were carried up the narrow entry.

"It looks like it's going to be a good bash," I said, closing the door.

I went back into the kitchen, made some hot chocolate, opened a box of my favourite Earl Grey & Lemon Tea Truffles by Hope and Greenwood, and gave Blythe and Elvira a Bonio each. Then I returned to the Bette Davies film I'd been watching snippets of for ages, snuggled on our old sofa feeling like we were living luxuriously and by comparison of a few months ago we really were. To be able to afford paint, food and posh chocs, not to mention an Alessi kettle with the little bird and soft furnishings was a delight.

We watched the film and then I set about having a clean through and did some ironing prior to another short walk before it was too dark. With Elvira and Blythe fed it was time to have a bath, relax and get ready for the party. It had been quite a social day already with Laney calling in and Elspeth and then delivering the candles over to Jock's cottage.

.

CHAPTER 15

The Party

Music could be heard as I walked across the green to call for Laney. She looked beautiful.

We arrived at eight thirty to a party in full swing. Music and a buzz of laughter and people talking. Pretty young people were walking around serving delicious canapés from trays. Jock bounded over to meet his guests and introduce them to people as soon as they arrived. He was an excellent host.

Later in the evening curries were served followed by a huge Eton Mess pudding.

Declan had not taken his eyes away from Laney since she'd arrived and it wasn't long before he was at her side.

"Tell me all about yourself," he said.

"What would you like to know?"

This was an obvious dance of flirtation that they were both excited by and they both disappeared to the furthest corner of the room where they sat on an old two-seater sofa that was from Ann's workshop that Jock couldn't bear to part with, and talked the night away as if there was no one else in the room.

It was a mutual interview based on adoration and intoxication with a heady sexual undercurrent. No one interrupted them.

Meanwhile the party went on, I met many interesting people, and it was good to hear Ted, Hugo and Oscar play their guitars together. I could see Ann in all of them.

I stayed longer than I intended because I was having such a good time and Laney came over to me at midnight to say good night. Declan left with her saying he was going to walk her home, which raised a few eyebrows and caused a few people to smirk knowing Laney only lived three doors away and most people being aware of Declan's amorous reputation.

However, he was back within two minutes looking quite crestfallen.

Jock joked. "Back so soon?"

"Yes, she thanked me kissed me on the cheek and shut the door."

"Not your usual conquest then?" Jock laughed and gave him a drink.

"I need to ask her to have dinner with me. Oh hell, I didn't ask her for her number."

"I'm sure you'll find a way after all you've been talking to her all night long, you must know where she works, ring her there," advised Jock.

"It wouldn't be appropriate for me to give you her home number without asking her first," said Jock, knowing what the next question would be.

I was amused to hear all this and I was so glad that Laney hadn't invited him in.

I thanked Jock for a lovely party, said my goodbyes and left. It was a full moon and the whole green and the houses were bathed in light.

Elvira and Blythe greeted me sleepily and we all went up the stairs to bed.

Meanwhile the party went on. Babs had turned up to complain about the noise but she was drunker than the majority of Jock's guests and was obviously piqued that she hadn't been invited.

Jock turned to the room and said, "schhhhhhhhhhh please this woman needs her beauty sleep," to which several people replied raucously, "It's too bloody late mate!"

"Apologies Mrs Smythe, we shall endeavour to be quieter, night, night," and he closed the door.

One of the guests, a producer of animated films shouted. "Wow, its The Bakelite Girl!" and then literally fell into fits of laughter and off the chair he was sitting on

The party continued the same as before. Declan had reverted to form and was very drunk and had already threatened to hit someone who had referred to Laney as a babe. As in, "Who was that babe you were talking to?"

Jock had sorted this out by announcing to the room that Declan was in love and 'the babe' was his intended.

And strangely everyone knew this was true.

Seconds later Declan had his arms around the man he had threatened to hit, apologising as was his way. Anyone who knew him well knew this to be normal behaviour for Declan, so they generally took little offense. Declan was always charmingly, profoundly apologetic.

Declan's drinking could go either way: sometimes he could be hilarious when drunk and lots of fun, but in seconds this could change.

He was a kind, generous, intense and occasionally volatile man. His personality was challenging, but he was a firm friend to those that knew him well but his intimate relationships were generally a disaster.

He was one of the last to leave the party and he was very drunk when he sat on the green just looking at what he presumed was Laney's bedroom window. He lay on the dewy cold grass and smiled getting to his feet as his ordered taxi arrived.

The driver's heart sank when he saw the state Declan was in. Declan was a man whose reputation went before him too and the driver knew he'd pulled the short straw for this journey.

The following morning Jock and the boys were clearing up when Declan arrived to help and to take them out to a pub lunch by way of saying thank you.

Usually Declan would lay low after a drinking session so Jock and his boys accepted his luncheon invitation knowing that he'd arrived so early in the morning looking well groomed, all things considered in the hope of seeing Laney.

However she'd set off early to catch an early train to London to view an exhibition at the Victoria and Albert Museum, where she liked to have lunch and people watch.

I had received a little note through my door from Laney inviting me to supper one evening during the following week and she had telephoned me later in the morning to say how surprised she was to find Black Bird Cottage all closed up with no sound from Blythe and Elvira and through a tiny gap in the garage doors she could see that the dear old Citroen van was gone.

Laney had thought how keen I was to get back to work so early on a Sunday morning. She was impressed and curious.

A little while earlier Rosalind thought she should be putting more water in her bedtime whisky when she saw a red Jaguar XK150 'S' following Louisa's classic van slowly up the lane past her window. It was definitely Louisa.

The Jaguar looked just like hers and tears began to splash onto the draining board as she ran the cold tap for a drink of water.

She really missed that beautiful car and decided that she was so hung over that her mind was playing tricks.

Laney let the motion of the train allow her to relax and muse about Declan Kelly.

She smiled when she remembered how sure he was that she was going to let him into her home and possibly into her bed.

It was a good party though and a memory popped into her head about a girl called Fiona that she'd known years ago when she was studying.

Fiona was a dangerous girl with the morals of an alley cat.

Dangerous to herself as well as all the hearts she broke and then danced on. Oblivious to the chaos she caused and only interested in the chase and conquest.

Wild and beautiful, sexual and fun.

This party all those years ago was at the house of a young farmer. He had inherited a rambling Elizabethan house and land from his parents. He had a blonde and leggy wife and a young child. Neither were at the house as his wife had left in some disgrace, taking their child with her. It turned out that she had been involved with a man associated with fraud involving a well known politician and her lover's case was in all the papers.

It was a wild party that spilled from the house into the gardens and onto the tennis courts where people tried to play and fell over drunk or were sick.

Someone decided to play charades and the game began in the huge hall where there was a sweeping staircase to both sides with a wide landing at the top.

Mark, whose house it was, took first turn and dragged Fiona up the stairs and into one of the bedrooms. Moments later after much giggling they appeared at the top of the stairs huddled together naked but for a white cotton bed sheet wrapped around themselves. Fiona held an alarm clock that said 10 o'clock.

They walked slowly down the stairs to shouts of "News at Ten. The Ten O' Clock Nudes."

Fiona gave Mark the sheet and it went very quiet as she danced back up the stairs naked except for a pair of tinkling Indian earrings. She was stunningly beautiful. An exotic flower grown on the roughest council estate. I'd been introduced to her family and they had grunted back in unison. Her father was scraggy and wore a vest that allowed wrinkled tattoos to be seen and her mother supported her ample bosom resting on crossed arms the girth of hams. Her brothers hardly caused a ripple in the gene pool. Mr Stork had certainly put her in the wrong nest. She never mentioned her odd home life but then she hardly talked about anything, she just was there and that was enough.

I don't think she realised how beautiful she was or what a powerful currency that was. She took nothing and gave a lot, literally.

Mark had coped well with his jealousy as only last week in a town pub, he'd discovered her out with his friend Robert whilst his other friend Tim, another young farmer, sulked over his pint of beer in a corner of the same pub lamenting that he'd lost his girlfriend to one of his best friends.

The landlord who was a real character and a bit of a charmer himself said, "She's always had a touch of 'Je ne quoi', the lovely Fiona."

On hearing this the now bitter Tim said, "'Je ne sais quoi', being a secret code for council estate!"

Three lovers in the same bar at the same time all ignorant of the situation was quite a hat trick, but Fiona had no conscience and could not understand their angst.

She arrived at Mark's party as his date whilst Rob and Tim were still feeling hurt and humiliated, though after the party she left Mark too and moved to London.

That party and the weekend it turned into was the last time I saw Fiona or heard anything constructive about her but I often wonder what happened to her and what she did.

Looking back, I still can't make up my mind whether she was emotionally damaged or just on heat. Talking to her, I realized even then that she had the attention span of a gnat, a butterfly on speed, as if she couldn't stop running. But she was very likeable and indeed easy to love.

The rest of us were busy studying. I was trying to understand bookkeeping and Fiona was simply too busy being adored.

Though Mark said that she did in fact stop and was still, if only to sleep. He said in a dreamy way that she would lie in his big feather bed and sleep like a baby, her luxurious hair across the pillows and on waking, she would look out of the large sash window at the end of the bed towards the fields and the cows and look so sad before reaching out for him. And then she was gone. She did not say goodbye to anyone. A noisy house with people enjoying lunch allowed her to slip away quietly.

After a while, people stopped asking about Fiona.

One or two determined friends did call at her family home only to be told to "Mind yer own bloody business. Silly bitch has left ome and that's that and about time too!"

Fiona's dad moved with all the urgency of a snail on a sedative. A master of lazy, slow living. A more laid-back life would be death. He even spat his dull words in a slow, slow drawl as if drawing his last breath. That the lovely Fiona could have come from these loins was nothing short of amazing.

So thoughts of Fiona slipped through cracks of time and memory as inevitably we say goodbye to those we love.

Laney also lost touch with the people of that time, being busy with her career choice and them with theirs.

She saw articles in the newspapers about Rob and conservation. Tim went into estate management and Mark remarried and became a ruddy faced successful farmer carrying on the family tradition.

On the Monday after Jock's party Laney went into work inspired from her Sunday trip to London. She had a spring in her step and was busy when her phone rang at lunchtime. In fact, it had hardly stopped all morning. This call was different it was Declan.

He asked her out to lunch and said he was downstairs in the gallery. Her stomach turned over and she accepted.

Declan was looking at a painting from the gallery's contemporary exhibition and seemed mesmerised by it.

It was by a Newcastle born artist, Malcolm Teasdale and the painting was called 'Fish and Chip Supper'. It was a family having supper with a whippet in one corner eating fish and chips out of the paper.

The more one looked the more detail one saw and the closer to the painting it looked like a blur. It was fascinating.

Declan turned to Laney and said, "I must buy this," and did.

Several months later this painting was hanging above Laney's mantelpiece as after a whirlwind and thoroughly passionate romance that began with lunches and candlelit dinners and picnics organised by Declan with furniture put into the car, not just rugs but a table and chairs and picnic baskets laden with food not least vegetables cut to precision to go with dips. There was champagne and sex in the woods and lots of laughter especially on the first night they slept together when Laney's antique bed collapsed.

It wasn't all idyllic though. Laney had caught Declan checking her phone messages on one occasion. He apologised and admitted that he was being stupidly possessive and jealous. He had also objected to her working late and sometimes being away from home on business for the gallery.

She soothed the situation by pacifying him like a petulant child but didn't give in, as her work was also her passion and part of her income. She still rented out the house with the student flats and shared the income with her parents.

There was also a time early on in their relationship when she had called at his flat at about 10am one Saturday morning on her way back from London. She had bought fresh croissants, Brie and apricot jam, his favourite breakfast after the full English and some fresh ground coffee and fresh milk.

They had spoken on the telephone early on Friday evening and she had said she would do this if she were on an early train so she was shocked to find the sight that greeted her.

His front door was open, fortunately onto a

communal corridor and not the street.

Furniture was knocked over, breakfast stools from the breakfast bar and a bookcase of cookery books lay on the floor. There was food trampled into the carpet tiles and smashed crockery and a trail of clothes and take away food boxes to his bedroom where he was lying on the floor wearing a pair of boxers and a tie. The smell was of stale alcohol and yesterday's curry.

He was asleep and snoring. She left quietly closing the front door behind her taking the breakfast things with her. She did not tell him she had called.

Their relationship continued and within six months, they had decided to live together in Laney's cottage.

Before he moved in Declan suggested they renovate the cottage. He would draw up the plans and pay for the work as his contribution to their home.

And so it was that Declan set about knocking down the rear of Laney's home just like the big bad wolf, he joked.

Whilst this was going on, they rented a little house just outside of the village. Declan had given up his rented town flat.

It was whilst the renovations were going on that Babs Smythe excelled herself in all areas of being a serial pest and the situation actually made Laney so ill with stress that she had no choice but to take sick leave from the gallery. This had never happened before.

Declan's daughter Daisy had dropped out of university and was visiting her father often.

She would sit on his lap and twirl his hair through her fingers like a lover whilst Laney sat alone and watched. These frequent visits always resulted in Declan giving her money, a couple of twenty-pound notes or more each time. Daisy showed no inclination to look for work. She would go out to dinner with them having sat around like a big bird in a nest waiting to be fed, a cuckoo, making no moves to leave and then Declan would insist that she stay in the spare bedroom overnight.

Amazingly, she always had a toothbrush but used Laney's toiletries, makeup and perfume. Daisy's own mother probably didn't mind but Laney did.

She never asked and just took. Laney had stopped leaving her lipsticks and eye makeup in the bathroom for hygiene reasons. She kept her own toothbrush in her bedroom too, just in case Daisy decided to use it or clean the loo bowl with it, not that she ever offered to clean anything else or give a hand with the cleaning up at the cottage.

Cups and crocs were just left anywhere and everywhere.

Fortunately, Laney's clothes were never going to fit Daisy. Daisy was boxlike in shape. A large box. Fat arms that wobbled when she raised an arm or waved.

The poor girl had gone to seed early.

Stocky legs that were incredibly short. So short it was a miracle that her huge bottom didn't bounce off kerbs. She had pendulous breasts with a cleavage that was permanently on show and expensively highlighted blonde hair that was naturally mouse. To add to the maintenance of Daisy were her weekly visits to the manicurist to maintain her false nails.

Sometimes she went to sleep on the sofa, Declan's sofa that had arrived with him. It was also boxy and red leather. Laney hated it but never more so than when Daisy was asleep on it with her huge derrière sticking up like a mountain.

Laney wished that Daisy had been a boy a lovely gay boy like Matthew instead of a spoilt daddy's girl.

She hated herself for being jealous but it was more than that, she knew she really didn't like Daisy and would not choose to have her in her life.

Things were not going well for Laney and we met a few times for lunch and a chat.

Fear had set in as soon as the cottage refurbishment began.

The contractor employed to carry out the work was a friend of Declan and basically took little notice of what she said, always referring any queries to Declan.

The work dragged on and on until Laney, at her wits end said that if things were not finished by a certain date she would be bringing people in to help as she had a good list of contractors having maintained her student let for years and her parents' holiday let in Devon that they used as a base when they visited England.

This caused a massive row and they only stopped shouting at each other when they realised that they were being watched.

Babs was standing in the yard behind a wheelbarrow as if it was magically going to push its self.

"I say would you move this contraption, it's in the way."

There was plenty of space but she was just being difficult again.

"There shouldn't be any obstructions here at all, I could fall over."

"Well if you fall into the barrow we'll push you home in it, now clear off," said Laney, quietly, like a woman on the edge.

To make matters worse Babs had had a hot tub

installed in her garden the previous week and everything had had to be lifted across the various garden hedges as it was too big to go through Laney's front gate or Babs's own front door. Laney's builder and Declan had helped with this chaotic event and had put up with a large pink van with the words WET LEISURE IS FUN emblazoned all over it parked outside their cottage for several days, not Babs.

They closed the door and left her to it.

"Do you want a hug?" asked Declan.

"No, I want my house back," said Laney who then just burst into tears.

"I know what we'll do; we'll plan a house warming party. Let's go up to the house, not daring to call it home and I'll ring the builder and push for a definite finish date."

On their way home at Declan's request they called into the Funnel & Gullet pub for a quick drink and all seemed well. Laney had even smiled.

On their way out they had a chat to Trev the Landlord and Sharon who seemed very happy, but on a seat by the door sat Barbour Bob, this was where he had been relegated to since Rosalind had had a little talk to Trev about Barbour Bob's attitude towards Sharon. Rosalind was a woman who always did what she said she was going to do.

A crinkly hand grabbed Laney and said, "I'm glad I've bumped into you two."

Laney removed his hand from her arm and asked why that was.

"Well I'd like to know what your builder chap drinks so I can buy him a bottle of something, he's been so good to my dear old Babs you know. What with cementing in her whirligig washing line and repairing tiles in the bathroom and then fixing the wardrobe in the spare bedroom, well the list goes on and on. Nothing has been too much trouble he's just downed tools and popped round. She doesn't know what she'd have done without him these past weeks."

Laney could barely get her words out quick enough she was so angry. It was pure soap opera like one of the cast from EastEnders when they air their dirty washing in the Queen Vic pub. There was a hush and no one moved as Laney's voice got higher and higher.

"So we are paying the builder a daily rate of say one hundred and fifty pounds and Babs is taking him off site to do her jobs in time that we are paying for and you want to know what bottle of drink to give him as a thank you. What planet are you on?!!!! Our building work is delayed because of Babs, it's us that should be getting a bottle of something to say thank you, in fact never mind a thank you. I want reimbursing. I want Babs to pay me for the time she has taken our builder off the premises. I'm going to see her now!"

"And you," she said to a rather shaken Barbour Bob, "stay away from me you imbecilic pompous old git."

Laney flew up the Street but Barbour Bob must have telephoned Babs to forewarn her because she wouldn't answer either the front or back door and her gold hag transporter was parked outside, so she was in.

And so when Declan caught up the argument continued in the cottage yard for all to hear.

"On the weekend that we were all hands to the deck barrowing in the concrete from the mixing lorry for the new floors, she came around and asked for help lifting a couple of bags of compost from the back of her car. Two small bags of compost and she expected us to stop work with the builder spreading the mix as fast as we could pour it in and you went to help her and gave me your full bloody wheel barrow. Every time I turn around, she's there wanting something. Or just watching me. When she sees you, she's practically got her tongue down your throat or hugging you. It's not normal, it just isn't. I told you he was never on site when I called. I said he was laughing at us, and so was she and you wouldn't believe me. You wouldn't listen! This job should have been finished weeks ago. It's been five months, our rental is up in four weeks, and I'm not renewing. I want my home back. Do you understand?" she yelled.

After Laney had left the pub with a speechless Declan in hot pursuit, someone at the bar was heard to say. "I never thought she had it in her, I always thought she was such a quiet girl. Spunky or what. Pint please landlord."

Barbour Bob was outside on his mobile phone in a panicky state.

He knew he'd be in trouble for this.

The next morning Declan and Laney were at the cottage waiting for the builder to arrive. There was a stony silence.

They put to him everything that Barbour Bob had told them and how they felt and asked him what he had to say.

He agreed that Mrs Smythe should have been paying and that her work was done in their time. Declan reminded him how beneficial their working relationship had been and still could be but what was he going to do about it?

It was agreed that he would pull out all the stops and finish the job within two weeks so that the decorating could begin and that he would work out how much time he had given to Babs and deduct it off their bill.

A letter was sent to Babs by Declan and copied to the builder about this and she was told to stay away from any contractors on the premises and indeed anyone working on the premises was forewarned about the antics of Mrs Smythe, the trade person's groupie.

Laney was still off work. She had lost weight and her right eye would not stop twitching as well her whole body aching all over and feeling very depressed but, this time off enabled her to sort out her own decorators and paint and wallpaper and soft furnishings and so on.

It also allowed her to be at the cottage overseeing the work every day.

It was one of these visits when she saw the builder talking with an electrician in the corner of the front sitting room.

She didn't disturb them and ran straight up the ladder to the first floor and into the front bedroom to answer the phone. She fell through the ceiling in-between two of the ceiling beams.

It was not obvious that there was any work going on in that area. No warning notice, no tools. Just removed boards under plaster.

The shock was intense. She froze. It was as if her body had shut down to cope with the pain. The next thing she knew was that she was being held bolt upright and rigid by the builder who had caught her before she hit the floor. She could not speak.

Her ribs hurt where he held her and then she started to shake and could not stop.

She was carried outside and already her body and legs were black, blue and purple. Her clothes were ripped.

The builder telephoned Declan. Laney just sat in the garden. Someone had given her a hot drink.

Declan arrived but didn't seem to know what to do.

Laney managed to get into her car and drive herself the short distance to the rental house. She really hurt but managed to crawl upstairs to bed where Rags and Muffin joined her whilst she cried herself to sleep.

The next day, there was very little to say. Declan could barely look at her, she was such a mass of bruises. She waited for him to go to work and then put on something simple that had no zip or buttons and required little effort before driving herself to the local hospital. She was x-rayed and was relieved that there were no broken bones, just fractured ribs and bruising. They said she needed to stay in hospital for at least a week to lay flat to ensure that there was no damage to the spine but she would not and drove home.

She made herself smile by thinking that the bottom had literally dropped out of her world.

She then made a great fuss of Rags and Muffin and promised them calm and normality soon.

Laney decided she needed normality right now and to be surrounded by familiar things so she rang a taxi and went into work.

Her colleagues were both shocked and pleased to see her but she wanted no fuss and simply installed herself in her cosy office and got down to some work which required little movement from her chair.

That evening she called a taxi and took lots of work home with her, which fortunately the taxi driver took into the house for her.

The next morning she was at the cottage early to meet with her decorators who were chasing the builder and his debris out of the completed rooms so that the cleaners could vacuum up dust and clean.

She had also booked a gardener, as she was unable to continue with the regular maintenance herself, a job she loved, so it was all hands on deck.

When Declan viewed the progress after just one day, he was amazed.

"Incredible isn't it? Laney said, "I organised all this and I haven't even got a penis."

He thought better of laughing and just muttered, "Well done, really well done."

Then with a big smile like a child said, "Can we set a date for the party then?"

"Yes," replied Laney, "the work being finished and my bruises being a little paler should be about another two weeks, so why not."

And that is what happened.

It was July. The garden was looking full and lush. It was tiered and had many little rooms that started from the top terrace by the front door. This area had urns, tall stone candles, antique seating, and a long table.

As for the cottage, Declan's plans had worked well. There was now lots of light and exposed brickwork. It was 'cottage meets loft'.

Between them they had endured a massive clear out. Furniture and pictures that were old friends from former lives were sold or donated to charity and whilst both of them knew it had to be done, it did not stop the feelings of resentment on both sides.

Eventually the resentment turned into acceptance and they enjoyed their new combined purchases. Well at least they said they did. I knew all was not well within their relationship because Laney told me everything. I was her sounding board.

Laney hated Declan's red leather sofas and he loathed her chinoisery pieces.

He was, however, always kind to her cats Rags and

Muffin, whilst Laney disliked his daughter with a quiet intensity and an insincere smile.

It had taken some devious planning to drip feed Declan into thinking that it was his idea to put a small sofa bed into the guest room and not a proper bed. And then the room was arranged beautifully to make sure that opening the sofa bed up would be a huge aesthetically displeasing exercise. Basically, she was sick of Daisy staying with them. Their relationship wasn't the same. They had stopped making love in case Daisy heard them. Being natural and without clothing wasn't an option any more. Daisy spent hours in the only bathroom, never helped with anything, expected to be fed and left lights on all over the little house along with dirty crockery and washing.

It wasn't the occasional guest that Laney minded, but Daisy the bindweed daughter as Laney thought of her. So the sofa bed plan was a huge obvious hint that it was time to go home. Still Laney worried that this was not blatant enough.

Daisy had all but moved herself into the rented property with them, little by little.

Laney thought it best to have a talk to Declan and Daisy about living arrangements in general to make things absolutely clear and besides Laney was fed up of worrying about it so best to get it over with and out in the open. And the conversation went like this;

"Well, Daisy as you know it's nearly time for your father and me to move into our cottage and start our lives together, properly as a couple. Now whilst it has been lovely," she lied, "having you stay with us so often here, you really need to be aware that that is not going to be the case in our new home. Although I'm sure on occasion we will invite you to stay over with us your home is with your mother or wherever you decide you want to live as an individual."

Daisy's mouth had dropped open at such directness and Declan was looking shocked and furious.

"Laney we should have discussed this alone."

"I don't see why, It's not a secret. I agreed that we should live together, I did not sign up for family living."

"We have your cats!" At this Laney laughed.

"Yes we do and they are just that, cats, not grown up people. I have, through choice never had children of my own so therefore I am not going to look after someone else's grown up offspring." She omitted spoilt, lazy, fat, and greedy.

"You cannot expect to throw another person into the mix now!"

At this point Daisy was mewing and tears were falling down her fat cheeks.

"Daddy, you said it would be all right and I wouldn't have to go home to Mummy."

"Oh did you?" said Laney.

"You are not moving in with us Daisy and that is final. Declan, we may be final too so let's have that talk."

She stared at Daisy who just sat there blubbering.

"Daisy, would you get your stuff and go home please. Declan, take her home and I'll see you here later."

"She's such a cow," Laney heard Daisy exclaim to Declan. He didn't say anything.

She heard them upstairs getting Daisy's stuff and then coming down the narrow stairs banging the walls with the accumulation of Daisy paraphernalia as they left. The door slammed hard and the car roared off the small drive. Laney reminded herself 'be careful what you wish for' and went up to sort out some paperwork from the bank for plan B. Her father had said that one always needed a plan and that it took a lot of planning to look as laid back as he did!

She felt a little bit sick and a little bit relieved but was frightened about what was to come. When she heard the car return, she gathered up Rags and Muffin and put them in the bedroom that Daisy had thought of as hers so that the imminent arguing wouldn't make them nervous.

But there was no raging anger just a stony sullen silence and a face that looked like thunder.

"I think we need to talk about this," said Laney. "I want to live with you and just you. There is nothing that has been done that can't bc undone so there is no point in continuing our relationship if we are expecting different things. I didn't realise that your baggage actually lived with you."

"Why are you so jealous of Daisy and I wish you'd stop calling her baggage," he said, and Laney replied that he was so totally missing the point.

"Daisy is your daughter and you will always have that special relationship, I accept that but I don't want her living with us, as I said I did not sign up to family living."

"You haven't signed up for anything," said Declan.

"At least I'm committed to this relationship; after all I've put thirty thousand pounds into the renovation. And I own the house outright and I've let you renovate it, so what is your point?" asked Laney.

He gave her his most charming little boy smile and said that he was feeling a bit insecure. He put his arms out and said, "Time for a hug."

They went to bed and had sex. The following morning Laney said that they still hadn't resolved anything and must talk.

He said, "If I asked you to marry me what would you say?"

She said, "I'd say don't ask me because just like my parents I don't see the point of marriage."

"Your parents aren't married!?"

"No. So what's the matter divorced Catholic boy, are you shocked?"

"So that's a no then," he said.

"It is, but I'm flattered that you asked."

"But back to our need to talk," said Laney.

"I have been thinking," he said.

"Daisy isn't happy living with her mother and I admit she is a bit of a daddy's girl, so what I'd like to do is keep this rental property on for her to live in."

"What a lucky girl she is, first a car paid for and all the running costs and now a house. I can't say I approve because I think to have everything given makes people lazy, however it is none of my business so you must do what makes you happy."

"You can talk. Your parents owned the house that you were a student in." said Declan

"Indeed they did," replied Laney, "but I ran and maintained it when they moved to France and furthermore when they purchased a holiday let in Devon as a business and for their occasional stays in this country I bought into the student let to enable them to do that because by that time I was working. And thanks to a small inheritance and some savings, I was able to buy the Upton Green cottage out right. It was a fabulous bargain because it was so run down. I'd say that was down to my business sense, hard work and a little bit of help from my Great Aunt Peggy, so please don't be offended at my refusal to apologise for my personal finances. So have you mentioned your plans to Daisy?"

"Yes, we discussed it in the car when I drove her home."

"Oh good, that's all settled then, so what about us?" asked Laney.

"I love us. I can see that Daisy has put a bit of a dampener on things, but hey, can't we just go forward now and move into the cottage, have a house warming party and get on with our lives. You know I love you and I'm totally committed, after all I did ask you to marry me."

Warning bells were ringing but Laney let herself be carried along, busy, moving into the cottage properly, though she had said that it almost seemed a shame to mess up the perfect show home effect. Then there was the party to organise.

Laney and I had met regularly and talked on the telephone most days and she knew my secret now, but I'd asked her to keep it to herself, though I would be bringing a special friend to their party.

I would have to remind myself not to be cool with Declan. It would be difficult as I was Laney's sounding board and knew their conversations almost verbatim. In fact, she kept me so updated that I felt I was there.

Laney and Jock had met properly in March at Jock's party and by September were living together in a rented property whilst Laney's cottage was renovated.

They actually moved into the newly renovated cottage the following April and the party was planned for June.

Things had settled down well and Daisy let them

get on with it and to enable this to happen.

Declan took her out for meals and gave her money. It was an expensive compromise but it worked and peace resumed.

Suddenly a couple of weeks prior to the party the honeymoon period appeared to be over with Declan behaving like a bear with a sore head and drinking a lot.

Laney had taken to putting Rags and Muffin into the spare bedroom and locking them in on the nights when Declan didn't come home until the early hours.

Laney was looking tired. Her sleep was being broken regularly. Declan seemed to think that she was his own personal concierge as he frequently forgot his keys. Once inside he wasn't safe to be left as he had on two separate occasions left gas rings on and burnt pans from a drunkards attempt at cooking. So she stayed up until he'd stopped ranting and fell asleep, his mouth open, his cheeks quivering as he snored loudly. He always had to have the radio on loud too, it was a wonder that Lucy and Jeremy didn't complain. They always said that they hadn't been disturbed but Laney knew that they were just being polite.

Lucy and Jeremy were having their own problems with Bab's frequent drunken outbursts. Tom Jones in the early hours of the morning not least Delilah wasn't everyone's cup of tea. And then there was the outside privy problem.

Babs had carpeted her outside loo in off cuts of the luxurious white carpet that was now throughout the cottage except for the kitchen, this being the main reason that she seldom used her own front door. Bab's outside loo was joined on to Jeremy and Lucy's. Back to back privies. Unfortunately, a leak had sprung from the ancient basin taps on Jeremy and Lucy's side and had sccpcd through soaking the newly installed pristine fitted carpet. Barbour Bob's stocking feet had sunk and squelched. There can't be many gardeners who remove their boots before entering an outside loo.

Jeremy and Lucy had been the recipients of more than one of Bab's screaming fits.

Both had refused to pay for the damage to the shag pile as they put it, as no one in their right mind carpets an outside loo, but they said of course they would get the leaking tap fixed straight away. As they walked away, both were giggling about the leopard print furry loo seat cover. They weren't frightened of Babs anymore, just tired of her antics and thoroughly fed up.

Babs had also taken to wearing Lycra leggings that flattened her large square flat bottom even further with matching tops always unzipped and on her feet pink and white fluorescent trainers. All this to attract Declan's attention. Most mornings she would run on the spot outside of their cottage front door before going through the gate and within minutes, returning. Babs had given up on Jock so now Declan was her manly obsession and weirdly he was flattered. They had formed the Babs and Dec Alcohol Appreciation Society.

Their alliance had begun after a particularly scathing objection had been placed by Babs for all the world to see, by way of the Town Planning department's website objecting to Declan and Laney's renovation plans for the cottage. She was not alone; Reg Beardsley was particularly affronted by the proposal for a first floor glass terrace, calling it a 'glistening artifice' amongst other things and every word in a capital font with lots of exclamation marks. Even Elspeth had objected and she is nowhere near the rear of any of the dwellings in Rotten Row. Elspeth did not want any changes made to any historic building anywhere; in fact, by choice she would have all women wearing Victorian lace caps and the men in breeches, though her objection was still a hurtful surprise because it would not affect her at all. She wouldn't even be able to see it from her house. It had to be a first floor conservatory because unlike Jock's they hadn't got room on the ground floor because of the easement.

The whole situation was wearing Laney down. To her it was a betrayal of friendship. Declan just laughed and said not to take it personally and that Reg Beardsley was a stupid twat, Elspeth a mad woman and he would sort out Babs.

Sorting out Babs meant turning on the Declan Kelly charm to melt down.

As ever it worked. A change of opinion letter appeared in favour of Declan's plans and henceforth Babs would have agreed to anything that Declan suggested.

Declan knew people in all the right planning places and their proposals were passed and the renovations began. Laney discovered that when they were in the rented house it wasn't the builder that Declan was calling in to see during the evening, but Babs and their relationship continued vigorously when Laney and Declan moved back into the cottage. For Laney it was a terrible situation. She wondered what the attraction was. What was Babs doing for him or giving him?

She was to discover the answer to this on the eve of the party.

Laney's colleagues were enquiring after her health, as was I. She looked awful.

She hadn't been properly well since falling through the front bedroom ceiling during the renovation.

Babs was still stumbling around ranting and being stroppy, ever more so since Laney had become tired and nervy. It was obvious that Laney was now being bullied.

Laney said to me that she hadn't the energy to fight back and she thought Babs and Declan knew it.

Things were becoming intolerable for her as Declan

was now having late night drinks with Babs. She would hear them in Babs's garden, drunk and laughing. She could see them from the glass terrace room. What irony. It felt like they were laughing at her and after all they had a lot in common, alcohol and anger. A .A. Ha Ha!

Even this little self-quip didn't make Laney laugh. Jock didn't have much to say to Declan, now believing him to have had his eye on the main chance all along, because seeing how he was treating Laney he couldn't love her, surely?

It was a good thing she wasn't going to marry him, is what Jock said. He also said that he thought Declan's behaviour towards Laney had changed since she'd turned him down.

Declan kept on asking how the plans were going for the party. Most of the arrangements were left to Laney. He said he would organise an outside bar, wine and champagne. The latter would be on a use or return basis from a friend who was a vintner and had a wine emporium.

Laney ran the decisions for food past him and he just said whatever you decide.

He had no intentions of paying for anything as usual.

There was going to be canapés, curries, rice, jacket potatoes with various fillings and a choice of puddings, Eton Mess being one of them.

Laney knew a good local caterer, one Mrs Verity Twigg. She was every mans culinary dream. Mrs Twigg had a fine nose for wines and a great appreciation of fine malt whisky and brandy and that was before she started on her knowledge and love of food. An effortless provider of culinary delights as if by magic. A short plumptious woman with shiny shoulder length raven black hair that was tied into an unruly careless bun whenever she was cooking. Tiny little well manicured hands and small fat feet that were always pushed into sexy kitten heels, usually red patent and pointy.

Lace from equally red bras could be seen as she always wore her apron bibs sloppily and sexily low. It was said that she had modelled for the artist Fernando Botero, not least for his painting entitled 'Bath' or for the artist James Mcnaught but she always looked coy and flattered whilst denying it. Mrs Twigg was a fearsomely intelligent woman, content in her own skin, confident, who remembered everything in minute detail, and hers was that sort of brain. She was married to a charming and hugely happy red-cheeked man. They had produced five now grown up children who when they were at school frequently had their lunch boxes stolen, rumour had it that it was probably the teachers. Verity Twigg was the countryside's answer to Nigella and everyone who knew her loved her and her cooking in equal parts, she was just that sort of woman. When invitations landed on the mat people usually hoped it would be Verity Twigg doing the catering and Laney and Declan's party was no exception.

Verity and her husband Tom lived with their children on a smallholding. They kept chickens and pigs and the children, four boys and a girl, were all part of the family business. George, the eldest worked with his father as they looked after the marquee side of things, the internet site was called 'PUT A LID ON IT'. Sarah their youngest and most naughty and artistic child, had a little business called 'LET'S GET LAID', much to her parents dismay. However, this worked well within the family business as she encompassed setting the scene for parties and venues from table settings and beyond. Sarah also drew and painted wildlife. Her favourite subject was hares. Some of these were for sale in Christo's shop. Such a talented girl, she also designed wallpaper and at Halloween sculpted the most marvellously ghoulish pumpkin lanterns that Christo also sold in his shop, much to the annoyance and resentment of Elspeth. The other three children worked out of the business in other useful areas such as web design, a 'proper' coffee vending machine business for events called 'Fair Trade Peculator' and in crockery supplies for catering, and all four still lived at home. Basically, the Twiggs had most things covered, including two converted barns next door to their own cottage that the children lived in.

Jock provided the loan of ninety metres of Ann's silk bunting and together he and Laney dressed the garden with it. Tables and chairs were borrowed from the church rooms despite Maggie one of the church women complaining that the legs might get grass and dirt on them. The table and chairs area were all covered in brightly coloured tenting from the local marquee company should it rain. A bar with a big glass fronted fridge for white wine and bottled beers was set up by Trevor from the Funnel and Gullet and he was supplying a barrel of local beer. Sharon was booked to look after the bar.

About eighty people had been invited, mostly Declan's invites to friends, family and business contacts.

Laney had invited neighbours, a few work colleagues who were also friends and one or two people she hadn't seen for a very long time who were travelling from London and were booked into the Funnel & Gullet.

Despite Declan's horrible mood and his insistence on inviting Babs and Barbour Bob and Mr and Mrs Beardsley, she was quite looking forward to the party. She had pointed out that inviting those that had so vigorously opposed the redevelopment of the cottage, not least the glass structure, the glistening artifice as it had been described from the plans, just might be rubbing their noses in it, as it were. Declan had replied, fucking good. Though he had repeatedly told Laney not to take things so personally. The garden looked lovely and the weather forecast was good for the party on the Saturday evening, although rain was forecast for the day before.

On the Friday as forecast, it had rained all day. The morning was grey and miserable and it was that really fine rain that soaks through quietly and feels like gossamer strands, light and quiet. It got heavier through the day building to a crescendo by early evening. Laney was really worried about the grass getting too wet and everything getting soaked. She kept running in and out to check that there wasn't too much of a build up of water on the marquee roofs over the table and chairs, and where necessary pushed it off with a broom.

She telephoned me that evening on my mobile, upset that Declan wasn't answering her calls. That morning she'd asked him to come home for an early dinner and to please not to have too much to drink or a late night because there were lots still to do on Saturday for the party. He'd told her not to fucking worry so much about stupid stuff and didn't she know how much he'd got on his plate at the moment. . She'd said that no she didn't know because he seldom actually talked to her anymore, but she had a few ideas. And with that, he'd grabbed his huge, scruffy briefcase and had left slamming the door behind him, which sent the usually complacent Rags and Muffin running under the sofa in the sitting room. It took an age to cajole them out. I'd already given my spare key to Laney so that she could put Rags & Muffin in my second bedroom whilst the party was in progress as Blythe and Elvira were going to be looked after by Lindy, the local animal sitter fairy godmother elsewhere so Rags and Muffin could have a quiet night in the cottage.

Giving Laney my spare key turned out to be extremely fortuitous.

Laney was exhausted, having just about got all of the party preparations under control.

It was ironic really; she didn't actually want a party. A house warming for a love affair that was stony cold. What was the point?

Declan still wasn't home at 8.30pm so she ate dinner alone and covered his with foil.

Rags and Muffin were fast asleep in a little bundle of feline togetherness.

It was impossible to tell where each of them started and ended, they were as one in their tiny wicker basket. It was so quiet the clock could be heard ticking and then the peace was broken by raucous laughter, then a groan and then quiet.

Laney put on her light summer coat and felt the coldness of the Black Bird Cottage key that was in her pocket from when I had given it to her. She closed her back door quietly and made her way silently into Bab's garden to the summer house where the noise was coming from and it was there that she saw Declan and Bab's, two players in a lurid scene, viola da gamba, she was held between his legs, his penis erect and in her mouth.

This vignette was an infringement on every moral fibre of her being.

She felt violated and sick as she ran from the garden. Time had stood still, she was numb. The journey is a short one from flirtatious exchanges to adultery and betrayal.

Declan had pushed Babs to the floor and had put his now limp and red lipstick stained penis back into his trousers and made his way as purposefully as any drunk to the cottage in pursuit of Laney. He was furious, managed to grab hold of Laney by the front of her dress, and pushed her against the pantry door, his face close to hers he spit out a load of abuse.

She pulled away, her dress was torn.

She shouted, "Just leave me alone, I'll sleep somewhere else tonight and we'll cancel the party and sort this mess out tomorrow."

"You're not going fucking anywhere," is what he said.

"If you try and stop me I promise you I'll call the police," she said, grabbing her car keys and snatching up the small baskets with the two cats in.

Declan said that if she so much as moved he'd take a fucking axe to her car and went to find one as his tool box was just outside the door since Laney and Jock had been using it to put up the party decorations. The axe however was in the woodshed but when frightened who thinks clearly?

She rang the police as Declan looked at her in absolute disbelief.

Panicked, Laney said, "My boyfriend has an axe and he is going to use it on my car."

Car and axe were trigger words to Laney; she had owned her white Mini Sprite with the chequered top and two black stripes with red edges on the bonnet for a big part of her adult life. It was a present from her father, and she reacted on impulse. Having given the details as quickly as she could she dropped the phone grabbed the wicker baskets again with the terrified cats in, they were too scared to move and she ran out into the pouring rain. She was shaking so much she could hardly get the key into the driver's door. As she did so, her jacket was soaked through and her hair was in rats tails. She put the basket of cats onto the passenger seat of the car, got into the driver's seat, and made sure all the doors were locked.

She started the engine, her teeth were chattering with shock and she moved away from Rotten Row keeping an eye on all exits with the motor running.

And then that stupid female thing happened, when we ask ourselves, What did I do wrong? Was it my fault? Have I over reacted? Will I be arrested for wasting police time? Will he have a criminal record now?

Laney had no idea about such matters and felt on top of everything else, really, really stupid.

Neighbours have come out of their homes. They were watching from doorways arms folded.

Within moments of these wretched thoughts of indecision seven police cars arrive, they have dogs and tasers. It is now apparent that axe is a trigger word for the police.

Laney was sick all over her torn dress. God, what a mess.

There was a woman police officer at the car window she was asking Laney to open the door. She did as she was asked and said, "I'm so sorry, I've been sick, he was going to take an axc to my car not me personally. There are so many of you. What have I done?" Then she just couldn't stop crying.

A male police officer arrived and asked if Declan was drunk and was the problem exasperated by drink and through sobs and a flood of tears Laney answered yes.

"We've got eighty people coming to a party tomorrow."

With a torn dress covered in vomit, mascara staining her face, rat's tails for hair Laney looked every bit the victim, and hated it.

Some other police officers walked out of the front gate with Declan. He had a small overnight bag in his hand.

He got into one of the police cars and they drove away. The woman police officer said, "He hasn't been arrested but we have told him to stay at another place for tonight. Would you and your cats like to go back into the house for now?"

Laney was escorted back into the cottage. It was a

mess, there was knocked over furniture and broken crockery. Laney asked the policewoman if she would stay with her whilst she got showered and changed and then she would go over to her friend's house and stay at Black Bird Cottage for the night with her cats.

Laney once more explained about the party and cried some more and remembered about being careful what you wish for.'

The flashing lights of the six police cars and one police van with dogs in eventually left as Laney closed the door at Black Bird Cottage and once more Kahill Gibran was right; 'Your House shall not be an anchor but a mast.'

She felt safe. Her own cottage was lit up like a Christmas tree as she hoped it would be a deterrent to Declan sneaking back in.

She didn't sleep but paced around making tea, black, as there was no milk, waiting for the morning to come.

At seven o'clock as the village was waking up she felt safe enough to go home. She walked across the green with Rags and Muffin in their baskets, but left her car locked in my garage.

Elspeth was watching Laney from her bedroom window, she had thought that it was I who had returned home and wanted to discuss last night's drama. Elspeth had decided that she would call on Laney in her capacity as the vicar's wife as soon as it was an appropriate time to visit, which due to Elspeth's usual craving for gossip would be at approximately one minute past nine.

As it transpired Laney was well in control of the situation. She had showered and had washed the rats tails that were the ruined result of yesterday's hair salon visit and a downpour of rain. She had also put on lots of makeup and bright red lipstick. The latter never fails when a woman is feeling really down. She was also wearing her favourite pale pink and black edged Moschino skirt suit that always reminded her of a condolence letter with a pair of very high black suede heels.

Laney sat at her desk and methodically rang everyone she needed to about the cancellation of the party, starting with suppliers of food (Verity Trigg). The wine merchant. Trevor at The Funnel and Gullet regarding beer, bar, fridge and booked rooms followed by everyone on the guest list.

She told Verity that she would of course pay for all of the food, but could she have the curries and anything else that would freeze for the freezer.

Laney asked Trevor not to deliver the barrel of beer and would he have the contents of the fridge back as the bottled beer was on a sale or return arrangement and would he please make out a bill for her for his time, appliance rent, cancelled rooms and anything else that was appropriate.

Whilst all this was going on Elspeth had knocked on the door and was summoned in by Laney who was pacing about with the telephone as far as the cable permitted.

Laney indicated that Elspeth was to sit down. This made Elspeth feel that she had arrived early for an interview and she looked rather put out. This wasn't what she had expected at all.

At last, the telephone was put down. "Good morning Elspeth, sorry about that I've got rather a lot to do today as you can imagine. She smiled and said in a very cheerful voice. I've just spoken to Charles, your dear husband and lovely vicar of this parish and have explained that the party is cancelled. I really am very sorry. Now what can I do for you?"

"I just wondered how you were this morning," said Elspeth, lamely.

"Coping," replied Laney.

Elspeth was disappointed, she was hoping to find a sad tear-stained victim.

At that point, the phone rang and Laney waited for Elspeth to take her leave. It rang several times before she got the message and then arrived home with her feathers ruffled cutting poor Charles off mid sentence, saying, "Yes, I know, the party is cancelled."

Telephone lines were hot with conjecture, assumptions and gossip.

As yet, Babs had not made an appearance but Laney had received a visit from a very angry cuckolded paramour, Barbour Bob.

He had not bothered to knock so Laney said, "Oh do please come in."

She wasn't worried that it would be Declan as after a heavy night he would sleep heavily and late no matter what.

Barbour Bob literally spat words at her. "He's there, the bastard, he's with her now. They've spent the night together."

"Well she was practising fellatio on him in the summer house last night. I saw them," Laney answered casually.

"Oh that bitch has no need to practice she's the queen of blow jobs and she knows it."

"Well known for it she is, the best ever. A lousy shag though, but one can't have everything. I love her." And with that, he started to cry. She watched as Barbour Bob blew loudly into his crisp white monogrammed hanky.

"I don't know what to say to you, I feel totally humiliated myself," said Laney

Saved by the bell or to be more accurate the knocking of the door. It was Jock with a locksmith that Laney had asked to call.

Jock kissed her on the cheek and asked what he could do to help

"Could you put the kettle on?" Barbour Bob had sat down and was staring into space like a senile octogenarian in a nursing home.

Laney asked the locksmith to change all of the door locks, which he immediately set about doing.

"Bob I need to speak to Jock, do you think you could leave us to it. I'm sorry but I've got so much to sort out."

"Ummph, you're looking a bit smart for a woman dumped and threatened with an axe," he grumbled and eyed Laney suspiciously, as he reluctantly took his leave.

His parting shot was, "Sorry to interrupt you in my hour of need. After all it is your chap that has ruined my relationship with my adorable, beautiful Babs."

On hearing the words adorable, beautiful and Babs in the same sentence Laney and Jock burst out laughing.

"Heartless bitch and Lothario! You make a good pair." And with that he left.

"Oh, it's good to laugh. I feel so terrible," said Laney.

"I must say you're putting on a good front visually," observed Jock.

"It's the only way, presentation is all. My dad always said that when you're down it's crucial to look the best you can."

Just then, four strapping young men arrived, Verity and Tom's sons.

"Thanks so much for coming; I'm so grateful to you," Laney explained the situation to Jock.

"I rang Verity and asked if the garden stuff could be taken away today and they're also going to return the chairs and tables to the church rooms, ensuring that the legs are clean she laughed and take down Ann's bunting for me."

"And now if I could ask you one very big favour," said Laney.

Jock sat down with his cup of coffee and said, "Ask away dear girl."

She smiled and said. "You sounded a bit like a character in a Noel Coward play then. So in that vein I'd like to tell you about last night's horrible farce. I was a curious voyeur of a libidinous contretemps. Or to put it less eloquently, I found Babs Smythe giving Declan a blow job in her summer house."

Jock almost choked on his coffee.

"To be honest our relationship has been pretty miserable since the honeymoon period ended. I think Declan likes the thrill of the chase, something new and exciting and I like a pretty ordinary life really. Also, he has some pretty big gambling debts, he hasn't been paying his bills, and this of course leads to him drinking more. I may have overreacted calling the police but I was frightened and angry all at the same time. If lasts night's argument hadn't have erupted, I was going to ask Declan to leave after the party. I was hoping that it would be amicable because frankly I didn't believe he loved me or wanted to be with me. And he hasn't made me happy. Be careful what you wish for. At first we were nuts about each other but I think it was infatuation and lust and in Dec's case, the thrill of the chase. When those feelings wore off, I suspect he asked me to marry him, as I may have been

163

the answer to his financial difficulties. I hate to say it, I know you're his good friend, but I think it's true. Since I said no to marriage he's been vile to me."

"What I wanted to...," Laney stopped talking because next doors front door was being banged ruthlessly.

She continued, "I wanted to ask you if....."

There was a dragging noise along the outside wall and then a slam of the doorknocker.

With trepidation and Jock at her side, she opened the door to find an angry, spotty young man.

"So you woz in then? You just don't want ta buy stuff from me!"

Jock and Laney exchanged a puzzled look.

"Was it you that's been knocking at next door?" asked Laney.

"Oh don't give me that. I've only taken five lousy quid all day. I'm trying to pay my fines you know. I mean usually I just go and rob another car and sell it, but I thought I'd have a go at this, well my probation officer said I should and the likes of you pretends to be out! I'm trying to get my life back on track!"

Laney was looking like this was the straw that broke the camel's back.

She took an audible deep breath and said, "Firstly the door that you were nearly breaking down belongs to my neighbours next door and they are out at the moment. Actually to be precise they've gone shopping at the farmers market. This door is my front door not their back door. The gate that you have come through is my main entrance, it is a private entrance and no one asked you to come through it, in fact no one asked you to call at all. Why is it always me, me, me, what you can do for me? I mean should I be grateful that you're interrupting a personal conversation, bringing angst and anger into my home and trying to make us feel guilty enough to buy your crappy over priced synthetic dusters by telling us the details of your crimes against society, that are no doubt all our fault. I mean, what are you saying exactly? Buy my wares or I'll rob another car?"

Finally Laney drew breath, but continued before the angry young man could reply.

"At this moment in time, I'm trying to get my life back on track too, but I don't suppose you want to hear about that. We all have choices you know, so why don't you go away and make some good ones. And don't drag that stupid bag full of crap along my paintwork on your way out. Oh, and here's a piece of invaluable advice don't get out of bed in the morning if you're not grown up enough to cope with rejection."

"Oh fuck you in your fuck me heels," he said and left dragging his nylon bag along the house wall.

"Things just get better all the time," said Laney and continued, "I was going to ask you if you would be there for us both, as a witness if you like, when I talk to Declan. I've texted him and asked him to meet me by the bench on the green at one o'clock. I thought that would be best, as it's neutral and public but a quiet spot. I shall be telling him that my home isn't his home any more, that he needs to collect his things immediately, which I'll have already on the yard. Also that I shall be giving him a cheque straight away for the work he did as an architect on the cottage renovation. I know how much his fee would have been because he's told me often enough. And I want to settle every penny that was spent on materials and labour by him, but I shall need receipts. I've already paid some quite substantial bills that were outstanding with suppliers and the contractor and I paid for the new furniture, so I think it should be straightforward. I want my solicitor to deal with this though, but funds are in place as I've sold some stocks and shares rather than have a loan."

The words came tumbling out so fast as if the quicker they were said the less it hurt.

"It's funny how things become clear; I now understand why the renovation was stop start. It was cash flow. If only he'd been honest with me instead of putting on that stupid act of the great I am. Now of course he looks like a startled rabbit in headlights with all the credibility of a back street car salesman. He owes money everywhere and hasn't been turning up for appointments and when he has, he's smelled of drink. I've been getting calls from high rate bookies too, as well as colleagues. I'm having to get my telephone number changed. Boy can I pick em. But Jock, why would he be sexually involved with Babs? When your lover does the dirty on you, you want it to be with someone irresistible and gorgeous, younger than you. To be everything you are not. But Babs, why Babs, he knows I loathe her, who doesn't, well except for poor old Bob? My street credibility has now hit rock bottom, people will think I'm such a fool. And do you know what music they were playing when I caught them having oral sex? Dylan, Lay Lady Lay. I love Dylan, I don't know if I'll be able to listen to him again. At least the track wasn't Magdalena!"

"Oh, bloody hell," and the tears began again.

Through sobs and running mascara she asked, "Why couldn't they have been playing something tacky like one of Barry White's songs, or Delilah, she's often playing Delilah. 'Why, Why, Why?"

"Shouldn't it be My, My, My," asked Jock.

"I know he's your friend of many years and I don't want you to take sides, I just need someone to be there to hear what is said. Will you do it, please?"

How could he have said no? At that point Rosalind arrived; she'd phoned earlier to check if Laney was okay. She'd said, "If there's anything I can do just ask."

There was and Laney did ask.

Rosalind had arrived to help Laney pack Declan's belongings. She'd even arrived with black bin liners, a roll of bubble wrap and a flask of coffee with brandy in it and some pastries bought from the farmers market.

She put the flask and the cakes down and said, "We'll have those later when we've done a bit. Now Laney, where shall we start," and Laney looked towards the Teasdale painting and started to cry again.

"Come on girl, get a grip now, worse things have happened, pass the bubble wrap whilst Jock and I get it down."

This matter of fact attitude seemed to work because the tears stopped and the three of them set about removing Declan's things.

When it came to clothes Jock just held the bags open whilst Laney and Rosalind piled stuff into them.

Quite soon all of Declan's belongings were neatly and carefully stacked in the yard all except for the Teasdale which was wrapped in bubble wrap, taped up and was put on the dining room table for safekeeping.

Just as Laney was getting melancholy staring at it packed and ready to be taken away, remembering the day Declan had bought it from the gallery. It was their first date, lunch, she had been so excited.

Rosalind patted her on the back, asked her to get some cups and plates for the coffee and cakes, and said, "You are doing the right thing, all you have to do is hold it together, no more tears now, and remember you are not a doormat. What has happened is not your fault okay?"

Laney nodded and managed a weak smile.

At one o'clock precisely Laney and Jock were

sitting on the bench on the green and watched Declan walk slowly towards them. Mr Darcy, the sullen brooding dark expression but no wet shirt or lake. Laney felt her stomach turn over. She felt sick. He really was very attractive, was she doing the right thing and then she remembered Bab's mouth sliding quickly off his wet and erect penis, her mouth open, like a vampire, shiny with her red lipstick smeared over her face.

Then common sense returned and Laney actually thought what a stupid woman she was to even think such a thing. I loathe him and she dug her nails into her palms some more.

Rosalind had advised pushing her fingernails hard into the palm of her hands, she had said it helped with nerves and it was working. She was also breathing slowly and deeply, she didn't want to sound hysterical or even emotional. She had been humiliated and threatened and it was time to move on.

The disintegration of a love affair interwoven with love and lies.

And he was going today.

Rosalind had stayed at the cottage watching the array of bin liners. She would be there when he collected them. Lucy and Jeremy were back from the farmers market and were also there for support. They were listening out for Babs, whilst talking about all the commotion last night.

Laney stood up and said, "Hello Declan I've asked Jock to be here for both of us, he isn't taking sides. I'm not going to go over the trauma of last night. There is no point in discussing blame and recriminations, but I do want to move on with my life from this moment, so this is what I have to say to you, I know that you are in trouble financially and I'd like to give you this cheque to cover the architectural works that you did for the cottage. I think you'll find that the amount is correct, as you did tell me what your fees would be several times."

He took the cheque, looked at it and put it in his jacket pocket.

"I have paid some of the outstanding bills for the renovation that you were being chased for and I intend to reimburse you for those bills that you did pay. I want to pay you for each and every penny that you paid towards the renovation costs. I shall need receipts."

She gave a piece of paper to Declan with the name of her family solicitor on. "If you present the receipts to him he will pay you immediately, there will be no delay. The new furniture in the cottage I paid for as you never gave me your half share so that is straightforward. I have packed all of your belongings, they are in the yard. Valuables, such as your Teasdale painting are wrapped and inside the cottage. Rosalind is there and she will pass those items out to you. There is no need for you to give me your house key back because I have had the locks changed. I do not want you to go into the cottage and I hope never to have to speak to you again after this morning. How could I have been so wrong about you? I thought I loved you, and that you loved me, that you were my one true love."

"Ah well," replied Declan, "each new time that one loves is the only time that one has ever truly loved, until the next one comes along."

"You heartless bastard!" said a shocked and shaken Laney.

"Let's go and clear your stuff out of my house. I want you totally out of my life. And furthermore if I have the slightest bit of aggression from you whilst we're doing this I shall call the police woman from last night who said she would come over as she's on duty."

He said nothing but just stood looking at Laney with a wry and arrogant smile.

Jock said, "Shall I give you a hand to put your stuff in your car? What shall you do, move in with Daisy?"

"There might be a problem there", said Declan, "I haven't paid last month's rent."

"Well you can now; you've got that cheque in your pocket, give the agent a ring now."

Amazingly, everything fit into Declan's estate car so he was away quickly.

Rosalind had handed him his possessions without a smile and Babs had not been seen or heard all morning.

The Lost Mistress

All's over, then: does truth sound bitter
As one at first believes?
Hark 'tis the sparrows' good-night twitter
About your cottage eaves!
And the leaf buds on the vine are woolly,
I noticed that today;
One more day bursts them open fully
You know the red turns grey.
Tomorrow we meet the same then, dearest?
May I take your hand in mine?
Mere friends are we, well, friends the merest
Keep much that I resign:
For each glance of eye so bright and black'
Though I keep with hearts endeavour,
Your voice, when you wish the snowdrops back,
Though it stay in my soul forever!
Yet I will say what mere friends say,

ROTTEN ROW

Or only a thought longer;
I will hold your hand but as long as all may,
Or so very little longer.

(Robert Browning)

Charles the vicar called in and over more of Rosalind's special coffee Laney told him everything and he just said. "Hmm, shocking behaviour and Mrs Smythe too. Don't let this experience make you angry though, think of the good things that came from it and move on, that's best, sometimes people never fail to disappoint, that's life. I always think animals are more reliable, please don't quote me on that. And now I must go home and be interrogated by Elspeth."

"It's hardly a secret Charles, that would be an impossibility here in Upton Green."

"Quite," replied Charles, "that is a relief; I may have been in thumb screws by tea time."

They all laughed and Rosalind said, "How about moving some furniture about and having a bit of a clean up, you know, change the bedding and stuff and make the place yours again? Come on, I'm not doing anything today. It'll make you feel better, I promise."

She'd already cancelled her lunch date and didn't mind a bit as she remembered what it was like to be betrayed and alone.

And then mischievously she thought of how soon the entire village would know about the illicit liaison between Babs and Declan courtesy of Elspeth.

Not that she wanted Laney to be embarrassed by gossip but it was inevitable.

She would see as much as she could that Laney held her head high and was not a victim, but everyone would soon know what had transpired.

The story would be exaggerated and twisted at every telling. For Elspeth this delicious licentious news would be a bountiful currency, it would be Christmas come early, an unconstrained joy to relate to the Gorgon sisters of the church flower guild.

And then there would be the visits to anyone in the village who had a pulse, to discuss the latest gossip in exaggerated delightful corpulent detail.

The tale would be embellished and have diabolist versions of perversion and would be told and retold over pots of tea and dainty cakes during the day and over pints of ale at the Funnel and Gullet. The post office would be buzzing!

Rosalind was keeping Laney busy and making her laugh singing 'I'm gonna wash that man right out of my house', and 'Another one bites the dust whist they cleaned and moved pictures around compensating for the removal of Declan's pieces of art work.

A mirror was placed where the Teasdale used to hang.

Whilst they were doing this Jock called in with sandwiches and drinks he'd brought up from the pub, courtesy of Trevor the landlord.

Laney said, "How kind," and started to cry again.

Jock looked at Rosalind, helpless.

"Hey," said Rosalind, "we're having none of that, of course people are kind, you're very well thought of. Come on let's get some plates and glasses."

When they were all having lunch Jock said "I'm really sorry how things have turned out Laney but I have to say it's a good thing you're out of that relationship because I've made some enquiries this morning and the extent of Declan's debt's are very serious. I had no idea how excessive his gambling addiction was, cards and horses. He has been totally illusive and deceitful. He owes thousands of pounds. He's always had a bit of a shopping habit, expensive impulse buys but his present situation transcends that into really big debts, but this transcends all that, it's bad, very bad."

Laney remembered him buying the Teasdale painting on his first visit to the gallery, their first meeting together.

Jock shook his head and continued. "He was always buying and selling his cars at one point he had a small fleet including a sports car a motorbike a camper van and a horrid beige caravan. I didn't know until this morning that his own flat had been repossessed and that's why he was renting. There was no way he would get a mortgage. I hate to say it Laney but he may have had an ulterior motive when he insisted on meeting you, and he told her all about the party that Declan had asked him to arrange. We may both have been conned. I'm so very, very sorry, but I thought you should know because it will help you get over him. He's about to lose his job too as his work has been suffering and going downhill due to the gambling addiction, drinking and subsequent worries. People are after him, you are well out of it. Get your phone number changed and make sure you ring the council to tell them he has left regarding community charges and electoral roles etcetera. It's a good thing you've had your locks changed. You should inform the post office too, about his mail. And I'm really sorry Laney but there is something else you should be aware of, he has been seen a couple of times in town at a cash point with Babs Smythe. She was the one withdrawing money and then handing it to him and they seemed pretty close. It would be hard to miss that woman anywhere she's so garish, practically pantomime dame."

"Well," said Laney with a deep sigh, "this is

certainly a pantomime. Prince Charming went bad," and laughed.

"I've lost a lover and you've lost a friend and Babs has gained another paramour, poor Barbour Bob," she continued.

"Ann never liked Declan you know, she was never wrong about people, never," said Jock looking bereft.

"Okay you two that's enough melancholy, Ann would expect you both to get up and move on and on her behalf I'm going to see you do. Jock will you give us a hand to move the bed around and turn the mattress? And Laney, how about we three have some of Mrs Twiggs's wonderful curry tonight? I've got a splendid fruit crumble already made and we could open a bottle of something nice."

All three agreed. By the end of the day the cottage was gleaming, furniture had been rearranged and there was no trace of Declan Kelly, even photographs of him and Laney and Declan as a couple had been removed from the computer and memory sticks.

Elspeth had called but Rosalind didn't allow either one of her big clown feet over the threshold and told her in a very Dickensian way that Laney wasn't receiving visitors at the moment.

"I shall pray for her," she said.

"Only if you've time," replied Rosalind.

Elspeth had already called at Bab's cottage and there was no reply, yet it was obvious she was in as there was steam coming from the kettle; she could see it as she pressed her large nose to the window.

Lucy and Jeremy had battened down the hatches and were spending the day quietly at home out of the way of any more drama at the very end of their garden in their summer house with their hens clucking and a few back issues of the RHS magazine and The Lady.

Gentler times, gentler times.

Jane and Freddie Harvey were away on holiday but Elspeth probably wouldn't have called on them as they really did do good works. As well as their day job with troubled children, they did charity work for the homeless. They had plenty of contact with those people young and old suffering from drug and alcohol abuse that they kept themselves very much to themselves. Dealings with Babs would have been like bringing work home.

Rosalind had noticed that people were walking very slowly past the cottage trying to look in. She even saw Reg Beardsley having a peek.

That evening before dinner, the three of them went to the Funnel and Gullet. Rosalind thought it best to tackle things head on so it was important for Laney to be seen out and about as was normal. Laney thanked Trevor and Sharon for the sandwiches and when a very drunken Barbour Bob asked Laney where that bastard boyfriend of hers was she replied. "Who?" Turned her back and continued talking. Just at that moment Babs's monstrous gold four by four slowed down and she was trying to catch the attention of Barbour Bob. It did. He shouted out very loudly, "Oh look, it's the Wicked Witch of the North in her gas guzzling chariot!"

She accelerated and with a screech of tyres and the smell of rubber, drove off at speed, just in time to be seen by Reg Beardsley with a gaggle of small colourful children.

He said. "Someone should do something about that woman, she's an absolute danger. She could have run us down! It's not funny, you lot."

He walked away indignantly.

Laney, Jock and Rosalind could hardly stop laughing all the way back to Laney's cottage.

Surprisingly it was a very good night, Ann would have been proud.

Jock asked if Laney liked the renovation and she said, "Yes, but there are a couple of things that could have been done better, a little more sympathetically, less urban. I think as an architect Declan always seemed to take the municipal route, which of course were the areas where he won awards at the start of his career. I'm not sure that he really understood old buildings. I retrieved a few lovely old things that he'd thrown into the skip one day and thereafter I checked everything. He also wanted to replace the old white sanitary wear with cheap Chinese stuff that a contact of his imported. I came home one day to a kitchen tap that resembled a hooker pipe. Fortunately, the plumber was still there and I asked him to remove it. That was another bit of tat from one of Declan's dubious contacts."

Rosalind talked about her marriage to Johnnie and their breakup. She told them some really funny stories like the time she left him swinging on a five bar gate. They had been having a row and he stood in the middle of the drive trying to stop her leaving, by which time 'the red mist had come down' and she pressed the accelerator of her beloved Jaguar XK150 "S" Roadster and he just managed to jump out of the way onto the swinging gate as she roared past in a cloud of dust and gravel.

And on another occasion when she had dropped the girls off at the home of Johnnie and his girlfriend, Miss Open All Hours she had let herself in and waited for them to return from work, in her case a cosmetics counter at Harrods, hence the nickname

Miss Open All Hours Rosalind had settled the girls down with some sandwiches and colouring books and had set about amusing herself.

Under the sink, she had found a can of antimate. This was a strange thing to find as far as she knew there were no animals in the flat and certainly nothing that needed protection from amorous encounters. It's a pity she never bought any for Johnnie though, still too late now.

She walked purposefully up to their bedroom and at this point Rosalind pointed out to Laney and Jock how silly it was for them to have given her a key to the flat.

Laney and Jock were just waiting for the tale to continue. They were not disappointed.

Rosalind had sprayed all of Miss Open All Hours knicker gussets with antimate.

She put the empty tin back in the cupboard under the sink.

She then found a new razor blade and selected a few dresses and skirts from her side of the built in wardrobes and set about very carefully unpicking bits of hems and seams, just enough to be really annoying but not enough to make anyone imagine foul play. Then she found some prawns in the freezer and stitched some of those into the hem of a coat hanging in the closet by the front door.

Rosalind said how much better she had felt at the time. Laney and Jock laughed but were a little bit shocked and surprised.

"Were you ever found out?"

"Not as far as I know and I could hardly ask and they never asked for the return of my key, mind you that would have been awkward because of the children staying there so often. I sent them to London during the summer holidays, you know, with a list of culture to experience. I kept Miss Open All Hours busy all hours."

"Why didn't you sabotage Johnnie's clothes?" asked Jock.

"Because although I would never have had him back and really have never forgiven him his betrayal, quite simply I still loved him. I came to quite like Miss Open All Hours too over the years and besides I quite like this present life of mine and I've had one or two!"

"What do you mean?" asked Laney.

And before she could answer Jock asked, "Did you ever find out what the antimate spray was for?"

"Oh yes, quite by chance. I was there one day collecting the girls when I heard Johnnie cussing about the bloody wretched squirrels. And why was the stupid fucking antimate spray empty? It transpired that they had had some new glass panes installed and as they were on the ground floor, they were being bothered by squirrels who loved the putty and as soon as it was put in, they pulled it out with their industrious little hands. Someone had told Johnnie that they didn't like antimate spray. I could hardly say that he should be content and indeed grateful that dear Miss Open All Hours would never be shagged by a squirrel."

At this, they all fell about laughing. "What do you mean about having more than one life?" asked Laney, when they'd all stopped laughing.

"We all have moments in time that are from different lives. If you'd visited me thirty years ago, you would have found someone quite different. Married with children and supportive of my husband's career. Then there was the life where I was bringing up my children alone, struggling and trying to make ends meet and coping with the break up of my marriage. I was also doing all sorts of courses trying to find something that I could do as a job that would bring more money in. There was the me before Johnnie, single and having a fun time. Then there is the me now. So many different lives. I have never felt more content than the one I have now. I am content, happy in my own skin even if it isn't as supple as it once was. I don't have the responsibility of my daughters, they have their own lives and I have so many interests."

"Do you mean your clubs and committees?" asked Jock.

"Oh, I do get involved with those, yes, but I was thinking more of my lover and my little exciting trips away."

"Wow," said Jock and held out his glass for a top up of wine that Laney was offering.

"By wow I take it that you are astounded and perhaps think that I am far too past it for naughty liaisons?"

Rosalind laughed and said, "I have discovered that when one gets older it isn't what one takes off but what one puts on that matters. I am very grateful to Rigby & Pellar for scrumptious undies, Wolsey for hold up stockings, Guerlain for perfume and cosmetics and the few makers of elegant, pretty shoes that I force myself to buy."

She smiled and sipped her wine.

"Living in Upton Green and being involved with all the things I'm involved in, the many clubs and societies made up of gentle or sometimes the not so gentle opinionated rabid Daily Mail readers of middle England, for me are sometimes like driving at 30mph. Difficult, restricting and takes resolve and an awful lot of concentration. A large percentage of my contemporaries are beige, very beige. Its bowls and troublesome bowels, elasticated waistbands and their only adventures are adventure sandals, always worn with socks. I'd like to shake them up into this century, but it's hard. Such myopia. So I enjoy the life that I have here and spice it up with little mini breaks of pleasure."

Laney topped up her glass, intrigued and keen to know more.

"I don't know what I'd do without Lindy Lou."

"Bloody hell, Rosalind, you're into women, well I'll be dammed!" said Jock.

"Oh God", said Rosalind, "no, no, no, well not since boarding school anyway. Lindy Lou is a lovely lady who minds the animals and the house and garden when I'm away. You should meet her; she's a tall blonde rock chic. Sings and plays the guitar, loves younger men so long as they have muscles, long hair and a few tattoos. The animals adore her, she's fantastic."

"Why should I meet her?" asked Jock, "I don't have any of those attributes?"

"Because she's a good person, she's fun and she could play guitar and sing at your many parties. I'll give you her card."

"I couldn't do what I do without Lindy Lou", said Rosalind with a teasing look.

"Just what do you get up to?" asked Jock, typically direct.

"Well, I have a lover. His name is Mark and we spend time together. Mostly in London at a favourite hotel in Bloomsbury that backs onto The British Museum, very handy, or on a riverboat tucked away on a little island on The Thames. I don't like flying, except on my broomstick so we stay in the U.K. We meet up somewhere every month."

"How long has this been going on?" asked Jock like a thwarted husband with a strange smile?"

"Oh, let me think, about eight years," replied Rosalind.

"Why haven't you married and where did you meet?" asked Jock longing to know details about another's love life as it made a pleasant change from people being intrigued with his."

"Ah, a multiple question," answered a languid Rosalind.

"Should I make some coffee," asked Laney.

"Certainly not," said Rosalind and Jock in unison.

"Let us open another bottle of wine, there's plenty of time for coffee with liqueurs later," said Jock.

Laney was wondering if she was ever going to be allowed to go to her lonely bed with crisp white linen now facing in a totally different direction after todays move around. It will be like waking up in a hotel room, strange and disorientating, should she ever get there. And then thought, oh, what the hell, and opened another bottle of wine.

"What firm knees you have, such a strong grip," remarked Jock as he watched Laney open the wine.

"Charming, dear girl, but you must let me open the next one!"

"I will answer the second question first," said Rosalind.

"For me marriage is something one does once, after all I had my children and didn't want any more. And I loved Johnnie, still do, but I'll never forgive him his betrayal. We're still close and not just because of the girls, he's a friend who let me down, but when one gets older, you come to realise that one doesn't make the close friends that one used to be able to. Perhaps there isn't time to develop a history of milestones together. Yes, one meets people with similar interests whose company we enjoy but it's not quite the same, not so deep as when watching a person grow and develop through the decades, triumphs and hardships. I think at my age I am the finished product and happy with my life so there would be no point in marrying, I am not in need of companionship or romance, just some inspiration, innovation, shared pleasures and humour, lots of humour. However when I first met my friend Mark we did have shared history and we knew personal things about each other. Our first meeting was extraordinary"

Laney and Jock were looking confused.

"Let me tell you our story. Are you sitting comfortably and drunkenly?

"When I was young and just out into the world of work I was staying with an eccentric and religious aunt in North London because her huge house was nearer to my new secretarial job. Her name was Margaret Charleston. It would have been difficult to have met a bigger hypocrite. A woman of multiple and interchangeable standards. She was a widow on a mission.

"My aunt had a liking for the working man. The dirtier the better, though she actually married a banker. If there had been a pit in our bit of London, she'd have been at the gate at the end of shifts loitering like a stalker.

"However, she made do with the old Covent Garden, the early morning traders, porters, and the pubs that were open all hours. She would bring them home and take them to her huge feather bed and after lots of creaking from the bedsprings and shouts of encouragement and delight would spoil them with food. We were never short of vegetables or flowers. Usually produce that they'd supplied her with. No one ever left my aunt's flat with a full bag, quite literally.

"When the market was closed, she was no stranger to the odd young foreign waiter from local hotels as a stand in.

"Her social circles never met as far as I know. Sometimes she'd be saying goodbye at the door to one of her special friends and have minutes to get ready for one of her legitimate visits from our vicar to discuss charitable works.

"When Aunt Margaret realised that I wasn't confirmed in the church the wheels were put into action right away. I was already dragged to church on Sunday mornings and stayed to wash up from the communal lunch for the old folk that followed. The big stainless steel sink was back breakingly low. On one of these occasions, I was groped and chased by one of the church helpers, lecherous Percy and yet Aunt Margaret did nothing about it. The next time Percy behaved inappropriately, I didn't run I stood still and said, "Bring it on big boy." Intending to knee him in the groin or hit him with a pan and he backed off like the snivelling wimp he was, like all bullies do when they are confronted.

"I had confirmation lessons with a priest who was visiting from America, one Nyle Dennon. Aunt Margaret was disappointed that I wouldn't throw myself at him. She suggested I should because she said he was a good catch and she'd like a bonifide cleric in the family.

"Anyway, I went to church and attended the weekly classes and my confirmation date was fixed at our rather lovely church.

"During this time, I'd taken an extra job in a pub and was working some evening shifts to save for a deposit on my own rented flat. I'd seen a little mews studio flat that I liked the look of and I wasn't far off having the money for the deposit and a month's rent.

"The pub was fun. I was working the evening shift prior to my confirmation and Aunt Margaret was upset because I wouldn't cancel my shift and attend a supper with the other people to be confirmed, at the church rooms. I was probably booked to do the washing up. She said being in a pub the night prior to my confirmation was very inappropriate and she was disappointed with my behaviour, which I thought rich coming from the dear old slapper that was my aunt.

"So I went to the pub to work in a very short mini skirt and high boots. Remember this was the sixties.

"And this was the night that a person came into my life that was to become someone special.

"Michael Wickman walked up to the bar and there was an instant connection and a wonderful strong attraction between us. The pub wasn't overly busy so we had plenty of time to talk. Michael was based in New York with his job; he was a buyer for a chain of department stores. He travelled a lot, especially to London and wasn't married. My new friend was of average height, a lean build with dark hair that lay over the collar of his long soft black wool coat. He had blue eyes and smoked a lot. I was captivated by him and the attraction seemed to be mutual.

"The excitement I felt was off the scale.

"Michael was lovely and he had a terrific sense of humour. He offered to walk me home and together we crept up the stairs of my aunt's house and into my bed. Clothes were discarded on the floor of my usually messy room. It was generally hard to tell where the floor began and the bed started.

"To this day, I remember that night, we were good together. It was young passion at its absolute best.

"Michael being lean, was fortuitous as when aunt Margaret flung open the door at a thoroughly ungodly hour shouting , "The Lord Be With You Rosalind," and burst into the room carrying a new bible as a gift, Michael was half way down the bed doing something delightful to me, but because he was lean the bed looked quite flat with the usual stuff that was thrown on it and she just said, " Will you please clean up your act, this room is a disgrace, a health risk! Your parents never said you were this messy! Breakfast will be ready in half an hour and I thought we could have some prayers."

"I muttered, "I think my prayers have already been

answered. Oh God! Yes! Absolutely!"

"Quite dear," she said and we heard her descending the stairs, singing 'All Things Bright and Beautiful'.

"I think I smiled all day and probably looked like I'd seen the light to the parishioners who nodded approvingly in my direction and certainly, Auntie Margaret looked happy

"Truth was, sitting on those hard pews required a delicate touch not to endure a hot bruised joyous reminder of the hours before."

"Bloody hell, Rosalind, I never thought you'd talk dirty to me in a thousand years," exclaimed a delighted Jock.

"That's just it, don't you see, it wasn't a dirty little one night stand. I was so happy."

We both went to top up Rosalind's glass.

"Our friendship continued and we grew very close, even though Michael's home was in New York, where he still lived with his family who'd moved out there when he was twelve. Originally, he was from Shropshire. His parents used to own a furniture shop in Bridgnorth

"Michael was a buyer for a department store and travelled the world for interesting and unusual things. We would meet when he was in the U.K. And we wrote constant letters to each other at least once a week. God, how I loved the feel of the thin airmail paper and the distinctive envelopes. We would tell each other everything, from the minutia of every day to the most intimate of thoughts. He would bring me gifts of unusual things from his travels, Indian bracelets, throws and silk scarves. Pictures made from Papal leaves and intricate drawings on exquisite paper. Vintage clothes from markets and unusual accessories.

"I have just one of these little paintings left. His handwriting is on the back of it and I've had it framed. I've moved so much stuff; so many times even precious things go astray or wear out. My diary fitted in with Michaels extensive travels, every possible day and holiday was spent with him. In those days, it was possible to walk out of one job and straight into another. Love and pleasure always came before work and outgoings were minimal, the rent and change to feed the electric and gas meters and most importantly clothes, shoes, scent and lipstick. Aunt Margaret had given me a few tips that I have always adhered to: Always wear the best you can afford. Vintage and second hand is generally better than anything cheap and ultra fashionable. Never wear cheap scent or make up and always wear silk or cotton underwear. It was my Aunt who introduced me to Guerlain and gave me my first Shalimar fragrance and red lipstick.

"Michael always looked comfortable in whatever he wore. The boy had a natural style.

"I loved his long black coat, the one he was wearing when we met. It was so soft.

"He'd wear the collar up and his dark hair would spill over it. He always had a cigarette going, and was consequently usually in a haze of smoke, and this he also did with style being one of those rare people that smoking actually suited and strangely his clothes never smelled of stale smoke.

"Sometimes we'd have a cigarette fest and we'd drink whisky and smoke Gitanes and the ubiquitous du Mauriers in the smart red box with the lid and those multi coloured cocktail cigarettes, I forget what they were called now, ah, yes, Sobranie of London, pastel coloured with a gold tip or Sobranie Black Russian 100's, in my candle lit smoky bedroom of the newly rented studio flat. So small most of the space was taken up with a large bed, a bookcase, one solitary armchair where I would curl up and read Michael's letters over and over, a chest of drawers with a mirror and a tiny kitchen area that had a miniature

Baby Belling Cooker and a tall burping fridge. Never did an appliance make so much noise or cause so much laughter. I owned a flatulent peculator too. Candles of many colours were put into the tops of wine bottles, quite often the little fat bottles of Mateus Rose. We did eat too. Toast would be made on my then modern little toaster that we would put on a tray on the bedside table, have anchovies on toast, and sip malt whisky in bed reading poetry to each other. Autumn afternoons were the best for that particular pleasure. One of our favourites was the Chilean poet Pablo Neruda."

"Ah yes, said Jock."

Forgive me
If you are not living
If you beloved, my love
If you have died
All the leaves will fall on my breast
It will rain on my soul all night all day
My feet will want to march to where you are sleeping
But I shall go on living.

(Pablo Neruda)

"Let us raise our glasses to absent loved ones," said Jock.

Rosalind continued with her story.

"There was a little shack that called itself a restaurant that I went to even when Michael wasn't with me, which of course was often. They mostly served bowls of chilli and stews and customers took their own wine. It was a home from home with candles in bottles and scrubbed pine tables, no frills. I was so drunk once that my long hair singed on one of the candles as I leant over the table top to Michael, who quickly threw a glass of water over me and then couldn't stop laughing. Also, there was a small hut, literally a hut on the side of the Thames on the towpath in Richmond where you could enjoy the most wonderful pizzas. It was actually called The Pizza Hut. This was of course before the big chains and it was really exciting. We would walk along the promenade and look down at the winding Thames, past The Richmond Hill Hotel and then meander back down to my little studio flat in the mews just up from the Victoria pub.

"I remember those heady days, enjoying life's pleasures without the compulsion to analyse it. We were so carefree. One day I shall go back and stand on the cobbles outside that little mews building to revisit that time and allow my heart to break all over again. Yes, one day I shall indulge my foolish old self.

"And then along came Johnnie, marriage, duty, children and Aga love.

"My first AGA. That could be a little story in itself. She was a white one and was looked after by someone called Mr Flowers. The first time she broke down, I felt so panicked and was on the telephone within seconds to Mr Flowers. Johnnie used to joke that I probably wouldn't call the paramedics so fast for him if he collapsed and he was probably right! I've never been without an AGA.

"I'm rambling dears, allow me to get to the point, so sorry."

"Not at all dear Rosalind, we're enjoying your story and besides neither of us are going anywhere,'" said Jock

"You're too kind; I must be boring you rigid."

"Really you're not, please tell us some more," said Laney, she hoped not too eagerly, topping up their glasses again. She'd never seen Rosalind like this, in fact she'd never thought of Rosalind as being young or in love.

"When we met I was eighteen and Michael was twenty four. It was 1965, our relationship had grown from strength to strength, I'd never had such a wonderful friend. There was never the gender divide, we were equals and shared so many things. Four years down the line when I was twenty-two and Michael twenty-eight our letters were beginning to tentatively skirt around what we were going to do, we seemed to have arrived at a crossroads in life where a decision needed making. Would he move to London or would I go to New York? As I hated flying and loved London I was hoping he would come to me but I was flexible, I just knew we needed to make a commitment to each other and be together properly.

"The very next letter that I received from Michael took the decision out of our hands.

"Michael wrote that he had been diagnosed with terminal lung cancer. He did not have long to live. This illness came on so suddenly after being bothered by a chest infection and a hacking cough. He did however smoke cigarettes to the very end.

"He did not want me to go to New York to be with him. We wrote and telephoned. With Michael's letters, his brother always included a covering note before he posted them, letting me know how things really were. Things were bad and within three months, Michael was dead. I did not attend the funeral, I did not visit him whilst he was ill so I never really said 'goodbye'. What was to be his last letter to me was just a poem and a kiss with a P.S. Mind the ciggies don't get you too my sweet love, my Rosalind."

"May I ask what the poem was?" asked Laney.

"Not if it's too painful," she added.

"Actually it's comforting to speak of Michael with friends. Of course I know the poem by heart. It was this."

Stopping by Wood on a Snowy Evening

by (Robert Frost)

Whose woods these are I think I know.
His house is in the village though;
He will not see me stopping here
To watch his woods fill up with snow.
My little horse must think it queer
To stop without a farmhouse near
Between the woods and frozen lake
The darkest evening of the year.
He gives his harness bells a shake
To ask if there is some mistake.
The only other sound's the sweep
Of the easy wind and downy flake.
The woods are lovely dark and deep,
But I have promises to keep,
And miles to go before I sleep,
And miles to go before I sleep.

"Michael's brother who was his twin wrote to me a few times. He said he'd read all of the letters I'd sent to Michael and that he would keep them safe. He said he couldn't bear to part with anything of his; he was even wearing his clothes, especially the long black wool coat. I wish I'd had that coat too and I told him so and cried so much I thought I'd drown in my tears.

"I arranged for red roses tied with a thick black velvet ribbon and no cellophane. Michael hated to see flowers encased in plastic and the family said that they would put mine with their flowers on the coffin. Two verses, different poems written on white handmade paper was with the roses."

I love you as the plant that never blooms
But carries in itself the lights of hidden flowers
Thanks to your love, a certain solid fragrance
Risen from the earth, lives darkly in my body.
If suddenly you do not exist,
If suddenly you are not living,
I shall go on living.

(Pablo Neruda)

I love you.

Rosalind.

"Aunt Margaret saw to it that I kept busy; she even gave me her Dachshund puppy to mind at nights and weekends under the pretence that she was busy with urgent affairs.

"One can only imagine what they might be.

"Young Buster certainly kept me on my toes, for such a little dog he was feisty and had loads of energy that required lots of walking.

"One night when I put him to bed early because I was tired out with grieving he ate a favourite hand knitted cardigan. I woke to find him in a nest of shredded wool.

"Thereafter I decided I had to pull myself together.

"I found a new flat, bigger than the last with none of the memories, not far away but without the necessity to ever have to walk past the entrance to the mews and see those old cobblestones leading to the rear of the studio. At the bottom of the steps from my then back door was a small patch of garden and one day when I was at work and had no idea that Michael was there he planted that little patch full of red Geraniums and put more in large terracotta pots on the steps. Like him, it was vibrant. I couldn't bear to see it. I thought I would drown in my despair and tears. A new start was best.

"I found a new job as a secretary based at chartered surveyors in the city and one day when I was in a pub after work with some of my colleagues, I met Johnnie.

"I guess you could say that it was on the rebound but I did love Johnnie, just in a different way, however with our relationship there certainly was a gender divide and I couldn't talk to him with total honesty like I could with Michael, but we had a good conventional marriage, so traditional he had affairs and of course the one I caught him out on.

"And you know all about that and have met our three girls.

"But to return to the present and my new life, I was invited to a promotional event beginning at Paddington station by friends of mine who are in publishing.

"The launch of this particular book about steam trains was held on a steam train. The Mallard to be precise.

"I was holding my champagne glass to be refilled when I had the shock of my life, so much so that I dropped the glass and went as white as white.

"'Rosalind are you all right, you look like you've seen a ghost', asked my friends.

"And I had because there stood Michael a much older Michael, but there he was as large as life.

"Who are you? I asked him, rather bluntly. He held out his hand and said, Mark Wickman and who are you? I'm Rosalind, Michael's Rosalind.

"I never expected to meet Michael's twin and I certainly did not imagine them to be so identical. No photograph had ever shown the likeness to be so striking.

"He had the same eyes. Mannerisms, walk, everything.

"We went off and sat somewhere as quiet as it was possible to be and talked and talked. Then I remembered that Michael had told me that Mark loved trains whilst his own interest was cars.

"At the end of the day, we were reluctant to part so we didn't and that was the first weekend of many. Mark was divorced, his wife and grown up children had decided to stay in New York, and he now lives in London. He is a retired lawyer with many interests that keep him busy.

"We bought a riverboat together that we have maintained or we stay in our favourite hotels. We visit exhibitions and often lunch at our favourite place the V&A.

"It is an arrangement that suits us both. Mark returned the letters I had sent to Michael and he also gave me the long black coat. It now hangs from the back of my bedroom door and sometimes I imagine I can smell the scent of Michael on it. On the anniversary of our meeting and of his death I drink to him and smoke a Gitanes for us both whilst I wrap his coat around me as if I were in his arms.

"Sadly, I've lost the letters Michael sent to me. I wish I still had them, but I don't.

"I guess a part of me was always belonged to Michael and sometimes I think Johnnie knew.

"But there you are, life is ever changing. Fortunes, like lovers and husbands come and go, one has to take the best from every situation and move on.'

"And that, dear girl is the best advice I can give to you.

"I do have one tiresome regret that niggles away at me from time to time though.

"I had no choice but to sell my beloved 1958 Jaguar XK150 "S" Roadster when Johnnie and I separated as money was in short supply and I really miss that car. I loved it and do you know I'm sure I must be going a little mad because now and again I think I see it going past the house at odd times such as very early in the morning or late at night. I've even cut my bed time whisky down to one very small one!"

"I'm sure there is a sensible explanation, Rosalind," said Laney.

And the ever logical male suggestion from Jock was to keep a little camera ready at the window.

"I haven't talked about this for years you know in fact the last time I mentioned Richmond and Twickenham to anyone I thought they were going to be sick with fright. It was a strange reaction, but it was at one of your fantastic parties Jock, and she may have been a little drunk. It was that young woman called Esme who worked for Ann. Such a slip of a thing and so pale. I was concerned that I'd said something to distress her."

"There is a reason for her reaction to the mention of Twickenham as peculiar as it seems," said Jock.

"This is confidential. The poor girl was sexually assaulted in Twickenham when she lived there whilst at college and she has never got over it. That's why she's such a timid little mouse. Ann did her best for her but she's very damaged still. So any mention of that area would distress her, but you weren't to know."

"It's a very small world isn't it?" said Laney.

"Anyway let's have a toast to absent friends, to us and to the future," suggested Laney to lighten the mood again. We did and then we moved on to one for the road and one for the green.

Jock walked Rosalind home and I slept amazingly well with Rags and Muffin curled up beside me.

The next morning Laney woke up and felt like a weight had been lifted. I had telephoned her and she asked if I could visit that day if possible. I set off for Upton Green, I also wanted to see Black Bird Cottage again anyway and check on the plants and things. I parked my car in my own drive and before I'd got a leg out I was accosted by Elspeth, but I made my excuses and ran across the green.

When I arrived, breathless, I was surprised to see Laney looking so bright and rested. We had lunch together, curry from the freezer; she laughed and said she'd now only got seventy-eight portions left. We talked for hours and I couldn't believe my ears when she told me Rosalind's story and of her own rather sudden plans.

Laney had decided to put the newly refurbished cottage on the market, she was going to make an offer on a tearoom, and gallery that she knew was for sale, owned by a work contact in Brighton and make a totally fresh start, job and everything.

Laney's was the first for sale board to go up closely followed by Jane and Freddie Harvey. They, unlike Laney were in no particular hurry to sell as they had taken teaching posts at a school in Shropshire that came with a house, so their intention was to sell their cottage in Rotten Row and buy a holiday cottage in their favourite place, St David's in Pembrokeshire to let out for another income source and to have holidays in themselves.

It was all happening; Elspeth could hardly keep up

with things.

Babs had cleared out her cottage and had taken herself off to popular part of Spain to live in a gated community with other Brits of a certain age and circumstance. Glitzy villa and communal pool. Heaven help the other residents. Thankfully, the gold witch's chariot disappeared and was no longer a blot on the landscape and within weeks, the third for sale board was up.

Reasons for leaving, the Harvey's their new employment, Laney a business opportunity, career change and broken heart, and as for Babs no one really knows if she did actually feel embarrassed about her dirty deeds or not. No one actually spoke to her after the fellatio debacle, though Elspeth tried very hard. It was Barbour Bob who kept everyone posted, in a very bitchy can't wait to see the back of the old bag, sort of way. He was still tending the garden, for money now not as a labour of love, paid via the estate agent, until a sale was confirmed. He'd rejoined a dating agency paying for the Gold Service this time round and was hoping for top of the range lonely hearts women or just exceptionally desperate ones with money.

Rotten Row looked still very pretty but dejected.

Laney rang me to tell me about the visit she'd had from Declan Kelly.

Declan had called on Laney one Saturday morning. He had moved back into the rented flat and he and his daughter Daisy were living there together. Daddy's little darling had cut Laney dead in the village and had refused to speak to her let alone acknowledge her existence.

Laney had paid Declan all that she owed him so she was surprised to see him on her doorstep. He was smiling an insincere smile but still the look of a rabbit startled by headlights. In fact I witnessed such a scenario quite recently when driving home late at night. A rabbit was on the road staring in at the field of nighttime harvesting. Even I was disorientated by the glare of the huge tractor lights.

And that was how Declan had appeared.

"Looking for Mrs Smythe are you?" asked Laney. '"She's gone to Spain, without you it would seem. What do you want?"

He made to step inside and Laney stopped him by half closing the door.

"That's as far as you go. What do you want?"

"I've seen how much you've got this cottage on the market for. Without my design it wouldn't we worth that much. I want my cut. It's only fair; it was my vision, my ideas."

Laney laughed and said. "I've just thought of something amusing that sums up our sad relationship. I fell in love and then through the ceiling! We both worked hard Declan and it wasn't just your vision in fact I've heard it said that since you've been drinking so heavily, that you are, and I quote, 'misguided by delusions of his own ability.' Your award winning days are over Declan and I'm trying so hard not to attribute to malice that which can be adequately explained as stupidity. And you have been unbelievably stupid and reckless."

"So pitiful," said Laney, a little bit frightened to be alone with him but nonetheless she continued, "I have paid you all you are due and you signed the form to say so when you accepted my cheque."

She had slowly edged out of the door so it shut behind her because she knew she couldn't stop him from pushing his way in. She then made a bolt for the gate and the outside world. Where was Elspeth when you needed her!

There were people milling about and he followed her to the pavement.

"I told you that I never wanted to see you again and here you are at my home demanding money. I have no choice but to report this to the police because quite simply I am frightened. You hurt me badly and humiliated me with that ridiculous excuse for a woman, Babs. I don't give a toss how you feel and I don't care whether you end up in the gutter or not, you've had all you're ever going to get out of me financially and emotionally, so why don't you go and crawl back under your miserable slimy rock with your stupid, money grabbing, lazy little shit of a daughter."

Laney surprised herself, she hadn't realised the extent of her anger, which up to yet had not been vented.

She did report the incident to the local police, they in turn paid Declan a visit, and Laney never did see him again.

Jock ceased to have anything else to do with him so he had no need to come to the Rotten Row end of the village.

Laney asked Lindy Lou to come and house and cat sit whilst she went off to Brighton for the weekend.

Rags and Muffin were two contented cats, as they liked to be sung to and Lindy usually practiced both her guitar and singing when she was house sitting. She was getting more and more gigs now and was really good.

Laney intended to ask her to visit Brighton to play in the tearooms. She was going to have a piano installed as well. This was going to be a tearoom and a gallery with a difference.

It was time for a total change. She'd decided to sell the rented student house and buy a small holiday cottage to rent out not far from the tearooms.

Much to everyone's surprise Jock also decided to sell both his cottage in Upton Green and his London flat and had had an offer accepted on a charming mews cottage in Hampstead. He was gushing about meeting up with Rosalind and Mark on their riverboat and all the theatres they were going to enjoy together.

There was just Jeremy and Lucy left and content to be so until a small house with a large garden adjoining Rosalind's came up for sale. It was action stations and Rosalind and Johnnie agreed to help them with finances to secure the property until their cottage in Rotten Row was sold.

Rotten Row now had a full set of for sale boards. Bets were being taken in The Funnel & Gullet about which one would be sold first.

By this time, I had sent out the invitations to my wedding. It was to take place in September. I had kept Laney informed of everything that was going on in my life but it was news to everyone else in the village.

It was Laney who advised me to keep Black Bird Cottage and rent it out. She said it was the best sort of insurance and pension plan. So yet another estate agent sign was erected but this time it said To Let.

.

CHAPTER 16

Louisa's Reason for Leaving

Out of every difficult situation comes something good and from my horrid divorce, I had my adorable and most lovely niece Felicity. Felicity is like sunshine, bright and cheerful, resourceful and fun. She is also gorgeous and is blessed with a personality like the bubbles in champagne. Even when she's down she's happier than most people I know and when she's short of cash she still has her charity of the week to give five pounds to. In short, Felicity is delightful. Not trained in anything much but for the piano and the school of life, she has recently embarked on a summer career as an air stewardess for one of the typical holiday bus in the sky airlines based at Birmingham Airport.

Because of this Felicity was to be the catalyst of my life changing so totally.

There I was living quietly in Black Bird Cottage scratching a living day to day with small decorating and gardening jobs and tolerating the barbed comments of Elspeth when I received some emails from Felicity. Nothing unusual in that but one of them came with an invitation. It was to a new restaurant opening, called Clouds.

And this is how things transpired.

I was in regular contact with Felicity by email and

wrote to her one day saying that I was feeling a bit flat; I'd had a run in with Elspeth and was feeling quite useless when I received Felicity's cheery reply.

Blythe and Elvira looked up enough to say it's time you took us out you know.

I suppose I should be grateful that Elspeth doesn't have a dog or I'm sure I'd be followed on walks. She seems to have a radar and knows just when to pounce.

Elspeth sat on a chair that Blythe was curled up on the other day and bless him he actually pushed her off with his strong little legs. Guiltily I decided that our walk could wait for a little while longer and I read my emails.

Monday

My dearest, most loveliest Aunt Louisa,

Sorry for the delayed replies to your most welcome emails. I sleep, eat, change out of my pyjamas into my oh so chic uniform, work, eat, sleep!

How is one supposed to conduct a romance?

So sorry you are feeling rather flat, this is no good!

A large pot of Earl Grey and chocolate cake is called for in these circumstances.

I shall collect the latter from Christos & Ollie's shop before I visit you.

Is Thursday at 3pm O.K.?

Please find the attached invitation. You must come because you have to meet my new 'first officer' boyfriend, Ben who is wonderful. Ben's friend Jack, a retired pilot is opening a restaurant called 'Clouds', hence the invitation.

I have another new and fabulous friend who will be there whom you absolutely have to meet. She used to be a dancer at The London Palladium, all feathers and sequins, anyway her name is Bette Lavette and she's looking for a designer decorator so I told her all about you!

I hope that cheers you up a bit. I must dash and don the

threads for another night on the flying tin can to take a load of immoral chavs to Zante (18-30 escapades!), no doubt draining pints of vodka as I'm writing this ready to regurgitate their innards on take-off (Oh the glamour I trill) if only their parents knew what they were truly paying for!

Must fly,

Will write tomorrow.

Love, Felicity x

Tuesday

Dear Aunt Louisa,

Here I am again even more tired. I am just about managing to stay awake during working hours and am truly embracing the swing of sky-high retail.

How lucky am I to have only moments ago returned from a one hour holiday in the land of the Sphinx and the Pharaohs.

The flight was most enjoyable. I was proposed to by a very overly refreshed (courtesy of my drinks trolley) older gentleman who offered to divorce his wife immediately and run off into the night with me. Needless to say, I shall not be leaving my lovely Ben in a hurry to dash off with said gentleman.

I can't wait to see you to tell you all about Bette and her exciting idea that could keep you employed for months!

Honestly, Auntie you'll love her.

See you sooner than ever.

Love, Felicity x

Wednesday

My Lovely Aunt Louisa,

I need cake! My work rota has been nothing short of barbaric!

I was called off my standby yet again and it has been nonstop until now.

I look like a doddering zombie in heavy makeup and a cheap suit!

Must dash, I desperately need to soak in a bottle of scented oils. I doubt I'll ever lose the fragrant stench of a thirty-year old 757.

Love, Felicity xx

Wednesday

Dear Aunt Louisa,

I am ashamed! I took a chip butty to eat in the bath and I couldn't decide whether to have red sauce or brown so I had both. I am disgusting, the sauces ran down my chin but it tasted so good, as did the huge glass of wine!

Good night.

See you tomorrow.

Love Felicity xxxxxxxxxxxxxxxxx

We did one of our usual walks, Church Meadow today and no cows or fresh cowpats.

It was a bright morning and Blythe and Elvira were full of play.

The plan for the day was to sort out some unpaid bills, have a good tidy up, clean the van, and then prepare for the highlight of the day, Felicity's visit.

Afternoon tea was a delight and Felicity told me in great detail about her new job and friends.

"Honestly Auntie I can't believe the fun I'm having, well apart from the actual job and the puking passengers. We had a great big fat man yesterday with his tiny Thai bride and his fat body spilled over into the aisle. The only seat we could fit him into was an aisle seat, and I won't go into details about the extension for the seat belt. I wonder how they have sex? Oh, not a good thought! He actually had the brass cheek to complain because the seat was too small! The plane was too small never mind the seat and boy was he sweaty. It's not a glamorous job, it's not even well paid but the social life is fantastic."

"But Felicity, you must think of studying something. Time goes so quickly you know and you don't want to end up like me scraping a living because I studied later on in life. I mean my Curricula Vitae is so empty it basically has one line, Too Busy Being Fabulous! I am joking! The seventies were great fun but I won't pretend life has been easy.

And marrying someone to support their career and potential isn't the answer either because then you exist through someone else and would always be seeking their approval and believe me that is no way to live.

You've got such a lot to offer, after all a cheerful disposition is the gift we all wish our fairy godmothers had dropped into our cradle. Life is so much easier for the optimists of the world, irrepressibly cheerful people like you who lap up happiness as their desert and take the cruel rejections and downfalls of life with grace.

You have all the basic tools to find fulfillment and accomplishment in a career that is well paid. I don't mean to go on about it every time I see you but every year that you don't plan for something is a year not wasted but used up doing something for the short term.

Creative people are known for their playfulness and sense of humour you could do an art degree and teach art or the piano, you could even teach the piano.

I hate to think of you in a tin can in the sky pushing a trolley up and down selling drinks, tat and lottery tickets.

In an ideal world, our jobs would be so much more

than the simple basic exchange of productivity for capital growth and a way to pay our bills.

Work should be good for us, not bad.

It should make is happy, satisfied not sad. Anyone who enjoys their work will tell you, It doesn't feel like work.

I'm glad you're having fun but I'd like you to consider what I've said for when this contract runs out and you're without a regular job for the winter again. Working for the minimum wage in part time jobs is hardly worth working at all financially and existing on social security is soul destroying. I never want to visit the job centre again, it was so embarrassing. They have security people you know."

"I promise I'll look at a college prospectus, Auntie, but I really must tell you about Ben Lynton my lovely new man, I've bought photos. He's a first officer now but he should be a Captain by next year, exciting isn't it?"

"And Felicity, what will you be next year?"

"Mrs Lynton, probably," and she laughed.

"So you do have a plan then, you naughty girl, but that is a personal plan not a career choice!"

"I know, I know, Auntie."

Felicity tried to catch one of the photo's that was falling to the floor but I got it first. It was Felicity in a red spotted polka dot bikini lying by the side of a large swimming pool with a suitcase by her side and a cocktail glass with one of those pretty little umbrellas in one hand and an ice cream in the other.

"I didn't see the point in going up to the room first; I was desperate for a drink and a swim. It was one of our rare crew stop overs and every minute counts!" she said answering my quizzical expression.

"He's very good looking," I said and turning into Jewish mother mode, I wanted to know all about him and what his intentions were. At this Felicity smiled a very naughty smile.

"For someone that was really naughty in her youth, like you were Auntie, you do come over all straight laced sometimes," said Felicity, smiling.

"I know", I said, "but you're the nearest thing to a daughter I'm ever going to have apart from Elvira. And she's been spayed, you haven't!"

"You and mum say all the same things; do you share a script writer for wayward girls?"

"I give up; tell me all of your news."

"Well obviously I met Ben through the job and we hit it off straight away, we like all the same things and giggle about everything."

"It's not a serious relationship then, ho, ho," I joked.

"It's fun, Auntie, it's fun, remember fun, who knows where it will lead. He makes me happy because he makes me laugh."

"They all do dear to start with."

"Oh Auntie, stop it, we need to find you a man before you turn into a cynical spinster of the parish."

"It's work I need most Felicity, it's no fun being short of cash all the time."

"Ah well, I may be able to help in that area."

"You already did, you brought these delicious cakes."

"I'm glad I called in to see Christos and Ollie, they've asked me to help them out over the Christmas period in the shop. Anyway, back to my most interesting news. Ben has a friend called Jack who is a pilot and he's the one who is fulfilling a lifetime ambition to open a restaurant, Cloud's, hence the name and hence the invitation to the opening night next week. You'll love it; the décor is inspired, to say the least. The walls are shades of grey and the paintwork matt black and there are lots of photographs of early aviation and of film stars from as early as the nineteen thirties disembarking elegantly down the steps. Beautiful clothes and little dogs in their arms and furs, sorry about the furs Aunty. The dining tables are ash and the chairs have bucket seats covered in silk damask. There are chandeliers everywhere in various shapes and sizes. The glass-ware is crystal and the cutlery is by Jim Lawrence. The floors are pale wood and the tables are bare except for the cutlery and crystal. There is a bar area that has a fabulous chrome coffee machine, black kettles and a Burleigh design of black and white patterned teapots. The crockery is plain white and made by a small factory in Stoke-on-Trent. The salt and pepper pots are black wood and the napkins starched white linen. It's a small restaurant and seats about twenty-six people in the dining area, about the same number as a Douglas DC-3 Jack told me. The bar area has plenty of room for stand up cocktail parties. Oh, the food will be organic whenever possible, fish and vegetables, no meat. An elegant pescetarian and vegetarian restaurant. You'll love it when you see it."

Felicity finally drew breath and said," I thought you'd like the detail Auntie."

"Indeed I do, I wish I'd designed it!"

"There may be something for you to work on."

"Do tell, do tell," I asked excitedly. "By the way who did design Cloud's?"

"George did it."

"Who's George?"

'"George Pemberton who is another pilot, a friend of Ben's and Jack's."

"Is he gay?"

"No, Auntie, he isn't."

"George was married years ago but discovered he couldn't father children so the marriage ended and he doesn't seem to go for long term relationships. When his father died, he moved back in with his mother, Bette Blue Lavette, his married sister, and her Lothario husband."

"That's quite a name," I said.

"Bette Blue Lavette was her stage name from when she was a dancer. She was amazingly wonderful and glamorous by all accounts and had very blue eyes just like Margaret Kelly, Miss Bluebell Kelly founder of the Bluebell Girls."

"I'm amazed at your new found knowledge," I said.

Felicity smiled and continued, "George is very interested in all sorts of design, he told me that's what he wishes he'd done as a career, but his father encouraged him to take up flying and work for the airlines and that's what he did, but now, like Jack he's considering other avenues. Well actually more than considering, George is giving up working for the airline as soon as he can, well, if he can sort out pensions and when the new business is up and running."

"What does he intend to do?" I asked, strangely interested in someone that I'd never met.

"He's going to go into business with his sister and that's where you may have a part to play."

"I'm intrigued."

"Blue's house is a huge exquisite three story Georgian pile with land, lake and outbuildings. For many years it's been run as a Bed and Breakfast and since Blue's daughter's husband left her, he actually ran off with a local barmaid, she's been running it, letting rooms to people who live away from home during the week and stabling for horses with the paddock and it's kept the wolf from the door, just, what with George's contributions as well and George doing most of the maintenance since Bette's husband the rampant Lothario bolted. I must just tell you this, during the war, Blue's husband would fly across their land and drop presents of flowers, stockings and things for her. How romantic is that Auntie? The house has been in the family for about two hundred years. George was born to older parents, his mother was thirty five when she gave birth to him in nineteen fifty five, as Blue used to put it, apparently, just when she thought her useless biological clock had fallen off the mantelpiece. They had adopted baby Bette when they were first married in nineteen forty and the baby was really brought up by the grandparents and the then house keeper as Blue was dancing and George her husband was in the RAF fighting in the war. Bette is in her seventies now but you'd never know it."

"So many Bette's and George's. As a family they were very economical with names, weren't they Felicity?"

"Blue and Bette. Bette is George's older adopted sister by fifteen years, there was a lot of adoption going on in those days if you know what I mean. Baby Bette was left on a local maternity ward, her biological mother walked out and left her there a few hours after she was born because her lover wouldn't marry her and this was the second pregnancy she'd tried to snare him with, but he was a heartless individual, quite spivvy by all accounts and the baby didn't get so much as a backward glance when he collected his girlfriend from the hospital and left. Bureaucracy wasn't like it was now and the adoption was quite straightforward probably because there was a war on. Quite a fortunate abandoned baby really, going up to the big house to be adopted. Bette, the adopted daughter also became a dancer, she was one of a troupe of a popular dance troupe based in London. Our Bette is actually Bette Sinclair, former stage name also Bette Lavette. I know you will love her as soon as you meet her. George her brother is George Pemberton and that is the family name and the real name of the house although Pemberton House has been known as Blue's House for years and lots of people know the story about the gifts being dropped from the plane onto the fields below for George's mother Blue during the Second World War. George actually owns the house and has done so since a year after his divorce in nineteen eighty-five, ten years before his father's death, aged seventy seven in nineteen ninety-five, but it's Bette's home too and now they want to turn it into a business. Blue passed away in two thousand and five aged eighty-five. She died in her sleep having gone to bed, in her clothes, drunk on champagne. George says she missed his dad so much she used to anaesthetise herself on bubbly. They're still finding empty champagne bottles in the garden from when she used to hurl the empty ones out of her bedroom window. Blue didn't so much embrace old age as fight it. She had hated owning up to age not from vanity but it stemmed from a personally deep rooted superstition that known age can be categorised and brought with it the status or invisibility of advancing years plus some if not all of the related age text book ailments. She was heard to bemoan that since going public at a milestone birthday, never had she been photographed so much, all from the inside with tiny cameras or from under a film of KY Jelly for the scanning machine. Blood tests such a regular occurrence that she felt like Dracula's Chosen One. Arms with veins blue, black bruised turning to a fetching purple. The indignities of it all that eventually paled into insignificance. She would rant about how stupid Mother Nature was because you spent years satisfying crazed hormones as a teenager and young woman, suffering the welcome or unwelcome erratic in her case, periods only to embark on the nightmare bus of the menopause. And then having got through the madness and wet sweats of that condition and to be free of hormones and messy inconvenient periods, guess what, your sexual urges have gone on holiday, forever, just when you could have fun without the usual problematic consequences. To compensate she over indulged daily in Champagne, cream cakes and cigarettes and worked her way through quite a lot of personal money very happily."

I managed to get a word in edgeways and said, "I liked the sound of this woman. I wish I'd met her."

Felicity continued. "Blue used to eat lots of very good chocolate too, interesting things such as champagne truffles and rose and violet infused creations, sometimes in place of meals. She'd say that as a child she wasn't allowed it and in the war it couldn't be had and then quite simply that drooling childhood adoration of confectionery goes as soon as you have a purse full of money to buy as much as you like and require no one's permission to do so, so Bette was fighting back in a small sweet way, literally. Some of the beautiful old chocolate boxes are at the house."

"That's quite a background story Felicity," I remarked, having now got who was who, straight in my head.

"Blue and Bette are so interesting and Bette has lots of stories to tell," said Felicity, her face alight with enthusiasm for her new friends. "I can't wait for you to meet them all. And you need to know simply everything Auntie. Shall we have some more tea?"

So we indulged in more tea and more cake and Blythe and Elvira munched on some of their favourite muesli doggie biscuits.

"I see from the invitation that Clouds Restaurant is in the village of Alrewas, I know where that is, it lies at the confluence of the Trent and Mersey Canal and the River Trent. I had a decorating job there once in a house where the River Trent flowed past at the end of the garden and a really big and beautiful Weeping Willow tree draped over it. I painted an old wooden conservatory. It was quite a hard job, loads of preparation, stripping back and repairing before the paint could go on. It looked lovely when it was finished though and all through the job, the weather was good. Blythe and Elvira liked it too. It's so nice when I can take them to work with me."

"Do you remember All Saints church then?" asked Felicity.

"Yes I do. I remember quite a lot about that village, Elvira, Blythe and I enjoyed some lovely walks there."

"Well if you were to follow the road around from the church, eventually on the right you would find a secluded entrance to a private road. At the end of that little road is Pemberton House and grounds. And that dear Auntie is where you come in."

"How?" I asked.

"George and Bette want to do the place up and turn it into a proper small hotel with a conference room and wedding venue. The catering can be done at Clouds and delivered to either conferences or weddings, but the place needs some serious doing up. George is still working you see so he needs someone to move in and help with the refurbishment, a creative hands on person that will get stuck in and see to trades people and deliveries, so I recommended you."

"How can I possibly move in, what about Elvira and Blythe?"

"I've already sorted that aspect Auntie, George and Bette love dogs so that's not a problem."

"Do they have cats?" I asked.

Both Elvira and Blythe looked up, interested.

"No Auntie, they don't, but they do have plenty of rabbits and squirrels."

Blythe and Elvira started to pack!

"Anyway you'll meet them at Clouds and you can make arrangements from there."

The evening of Clouds opening came around quickly and I'd no spare cash to buy a new dress so I wore an old faithful Jean Muir vintage black dress from the seventies.

It was a lovely dress with lots of little jet buttons on the sleeves and a very flattering cut, simple. I wore my favourite black suede platform shoes that were as comfortable as slippers, grabbed a little embroidered clutch bag from the nineteen forties and I was good to go. I was really nervous. I made Elvira and Blythe comfortable and told them that I wouldn't be long. They looked at me with looks that said they'd heard that old chestnut before. I climbed into my trusty old Citroen van that I'd cleaned and valeted that day and left for the party.

When I arrived, the party was in full swing and I had to park a little way from the venue.

As soon as I entered the warm and exquisite Clouds venue Felicity came rushing over to me with Ben and George in tow.

Ben was lovely a really nice young man, but it was as if I'd known George all my life and in other lives as well.

We were inseparable all evening. He introduced me to Jack and to Bette and they were all that Felicity had described and more.

I had more fun than I'd experienced in a very long time.

It was midnight before I left, tearing myself away, explaining that I had to return home to Blythe and Elvira.

George and Bette, Jack, Felicity and Ben all walked with me to my van.

"My, what do we have here," said George.

"This is my lovely Citroen Acadiane van," I said.

"I love her!" said George.

And the very fact that he'd called her a he spoke volumes to me.

I promised everyone I'd be at Pemberton House tomorrow for afternoon tea at 4pm. I declined Sunday lunch, as it had never been a meal that I've liked, as much as I couldn't wait to see George again.

George said, "Come at 3 o'clock then I can show you around before tea."

I agreed, gladly.

And they all waved me off.

I drove home in a bubble of happiness.

Elvira and Blythe were very keen to go out into the garden and so was I to stare up at the stars.

My two little dogs looked disgusted with me and stood in a determined stance by the choc drop jar.

The chocolate fine paid we all went up to bed.

There was the usual click clack of people walking up to church for eight o'clock mass but we were all awake anyway and just about to go out for our walk as soon as the dedicated and good were in church.

I paid no attention to my friends, the dead, whom I pass by every day I was too happy for contemplation and thoughts of mortality.

There were no cows and the cowpats were dry. Our walk was untroubled until I saw Elspeth loitering on the green.

"I called round to see you last evening, twice but you were out. Honestly I don't know how you can afford to be out enjoying yourself the whole time, it's not as if you have a regular job is it."

"I'm hardly ever out in the evening," I said. "Anyway what did you want me for?"

"Oh, so you don't remember then that you promised to help out with the luncheon for the oldies in the parish rooms today?"

Washing up, low sinks and backache came to mind.

"I didn't actually say I would and I certainly never confirmed anything with you and as it happens I've got an appointment today so my helping is out of the question, sorry."

I heard her mutter as selfish as ever, but I didn't rise to the bait and walked swiftly on. Elspeth was not going to rain on my parade today.

"What sort of appointment?" she shouted after me.

"An interview for an old scrubber in a large house," I replied.

A silly poem came to mind, that was written for me by someone that I'd asked to give me a hand with preparation for a particularly dirty job.

Odes From An Old Scrubber

Twas always my ambition to be a movie star
But fickle fame eluded me, so I became a char
My leading man's a hoover
It's hard to earn a crust
Now all my hopes of stardom have vanished in the dust.
I longed to dress in cashmere

215

And smell of French perfume
Alas my props are dusters, mops, brushes a dustpan
and a broom.

A gift from Prudence.

It was an old cottage in the grounds of an old house for staff that came to mind. It was a Lady Lucinda, Lucrezia Borgias would have been more apt, somewhere in deepest Hampshire, that booked the job and a more mean and embittered stringy old harridan would be hard to find. Prudence O'Riley a former neighbour agreed to help me and I was so relieved.

The little cottage was actually very pretty; roses around the door sort of place, but inside it was pure workhouse. Basic furniture and single iron beds with thin dirty mattresses. There was no central heating or hot water and the place was covered in soot and smoke and grease from cooking. Before painting through with an ordinary white wash cleaning had to be done.

Lady Lucinda suggested boiling a kettle! Sponge mops were taken to the ceiling and Prudence and I wore scarves, visors so that the drips of oily black water wouldn't get in our hair, and eyes. I was secretly praying to myself that Prudence wouldn't let me down, dip into her cavernous handbag for her hip flask of whisky, and top herself up. She was a manic depressive alcoholic, but finding help was hard.

The unfortunate incoming staff were employed to look after Lady Lucinda's mother.

It was all a bit Bates Motel and we couldn't wait to get out of there. I actually asked Prudence to stay and help with the painting so I could get finished quicker and then because of this had to have a battle about the bill as the work was done quicker than the estimate because of two people working and not just one. She paid and it was a Coutts cheque, though she did write a letter of complaint to me and I in turn wrote one to her.

But back to the present. I dressed in another old favourite dress and a sweet little box jacket. I had brushed Elvira and Blythe and had brushed their teeth. I had packed food for them for later and just when I was reversing out of the drive, I saw Elspeth running towards us, so we left in rather a hurry and I watched in the rear view mirror, as she became a pleasant untroublesome small dot in the distance.

Elvira and Blythe were quite excited, they liked going out in the van in their mobile boudoir.

I was quite excited too. I couldn't wait to speak to everyone about their business plans and décor.

Pemberton House was large, impressive and welcoming. George ran to the van before I'd stopped and said how pleased he was to see me again and then made a great fuss of Blythe and Elvira.

Bette stood at the front door and called for us to go in. The first thing Blythe did was to run up the sweeping staircase and have a look round before coming down looking more aristocratic than usual, with a look of this'll do on his long muzzled face.

Elvira had taken a liking to Bette and was sitting at her feet.

Jack was in the kitchen cooking. George asked how long food would be and was told forty-five minutes, so Bette took Blythe and Elvira into a lovely sitting room with a glorious log fire burning whilst George gave me a tour of the house and gardens.

Over high tea, the four of us discussed ideas for the décor and business. Arrangements were made and I was on board and employed from that day.

For months, it was all systems go with hardly a break but whilst it was hard work it was a joy to be involved with such enthusiastic people.

George and I fell in love with each other on the night we met at Jack's restaurant.

From then on, we were hardly apart except for when he went to work.

We liked the same things, laughed at the same old jokes, loved old cars. I had never felt so at one with anyone ever. George, Elvira and Blythe had a mutual admiration society going. Never had I been so utterly content.

Pemberton House was going to be a Country Wedding Venue and a Boutique B&B with a small conference facility.

There were ten bedrooms in the house and two large bathrooms. As the rooms were large, it was possible to put en suites in most of them.

There was a ballroom and this was to be the wedding venue/conference room.

There were two cottages a barn and stables in the grounds and a beautiful small house called The Music House. The two cottages were totally refurbished and Bette was to move into one of them. The other was to be for rent as a holiday rental and George and I were moving into The Music House.

The barn was made into a multi storage area for furniture and wedding props.

The stables were already made over to garaging with an adjacent gravelled area that would serve as a car park.

There was a pretty two-storey boathouse at the side of the lake and a small rowing boat loosely tied floated gently in the water.

There were bronze sculptures here and there; one was of three life size women in nineteen forties clothes, running, with arms linked, holding on to their hats with their coats blowing open in the wind. There was a unicorn, a horse, and various stone statues.

The whole place was magical.

It was whilst George and I were thinking about clearing out the stables and had decided to take a break sitting in George's classic Jaguar sports car when he asked me if I remembered any of the Kenny Everett comedy sketches.

"I do remember some," I said, not least a very rude one with a clever play of words between Carla and the Captain in the space ship.

And together we recited it.

Carla: "I say Captain, what do you do to relax at the weekend."

Captain: "Well, Carla, I'm a country remember."

Carla: "Sure Captain, I remember, but what do you do for the weekend?"

We both had a fit of the giggles and when George had stopped laughing, but with a big smile on his face, he asked me to go to New York with him. I said yes, despite not being a fan of air travel.

We didn't clean out the stables that day but went up to the boathouse and made love. Then we told Bette our good news and phoned Jack and Felicity and Ben and Laney and opened a lovely bottle of champagne.

Felicity was absolutely delighted, whooped, and trilled with excitement.

The gold paper from the champagne bottle George made into a ring, playfully put it on my wedding ring finger, and then put it in his pocket. At that time I was on such a high, I didn't pick up on the unhappiness in Laney's' voice.

We had started on the cottages and barn because the house needed to be empty and we needed a place to store building materials and furniture.

The Music House required no more than a little cosmetic work.

Apart from the en suites, the bedrooms were an easy task and a delight to style. All were individual in that they had different wall coverings. We found some fabulous wallpaper, a Nina Campbell design of swans for one and an Osbourne & Little parrots for another. A real find was a design of Paris scenes in soft blacks, whites and greys.

With these strong patterns, we had the drapes made in the matching fabric so that there was no break in thc design when the drapes were closed and all of the windows were dressed with neutral roller blinds to diffuse strong daylight.

The design brief was stylish, simple, comfortable and uncluttered with a palette of gentle colours.

The woodwork was painted in soft shades of matt white or palest grey throughout the house. Floors were their original wood and tiles with runners or rugs.

The two large bathrooms were left much as they were with huge baths; one of them was a 1930's model. It had a step down into it and was an aqua marine coloured with a matching square pedestal sink with shell soap dishes and rails for towels and a loo with a huge wooden seat.

As for the bedroom furniture, the good old beds were kept and new luxurious mattresses were bought. Some beds needed to be changed and new double ones were purchased.

A lot of furniture was sadly sent to auction, as it just wasn't suitable for the look and feel that we were trying to achieve.

Olly and Christo helped with the styling of the guest bedrooms and the sourcing of furniture.

Where possible alcove spaces were turned into wardrobes with unique French style cupboard doors on the front and they were painted in the same matt whites and greys of the room. They were finished beautifully and were wall papered and painted on the inside too. Finish and detail were of paramount importance to us all.

Christo and Olly found a wonderful console table design for all of the bedrooms.

It was long enough to serve as a desk and dressing table. The base was of a solid carved Puginesque, Gothic revival style, heavily carved and the top distressed wood. Large mirrors of the same design were hung above the console tables.

Each room had two small felt wool armchairs with studied arms in a neutral putty colour with an occasional table between them, tall bedside cabinets with bedside lamps for a gentle light and adjustable wall lights in a distressed finish for reading.

There were rugs either side of the large bed and one on the hearth of those rooms that had a fireplace. The en suites were small but finished to the highest of standards.

The ballroom was a sight to behold and could easily be changed into a formal room for business conferences.

The windfall that George had acquired from the premium bonds just about covered all of the renovation costs.

A grand opening was planned. Invitations had gone out to wedding dress and wedding hire shops, florists, photographers, churches, businesses far and wide. Advertisements were placed in parish magazines, bridal magazines and local papers.

The web page was brilliant and the grand opening a success. Olly and Christo had decked the house with the most exquisite floral displays. Pemberton House could offer the complete wedding package.

A Wedding Fayre was arranged and bookings began to come in.

Fortunately, Jack had a very good little black book of trained staff and he took care of the menu and catering side of things in his brand new kitchen at Pemberton House and at his restaurant, Clouds. Bette had organised cleaners and gardeners and maintenance people and a part time administrator by the name of Louise had been employed. She was incredibly efficient and would probably be employed full time quite soon. I was in awe; there was nothing she couldn't do on a computer at speed!

George had booked the tickets for New York and Lindy Lou was asked to move into The Music House for four days to look after Blythe and Elvira. I treated myself to a couple of new outfits and excitedly we set off for our little holiday.

George couldn't wait to show me everything; three days in, I was exhausted. It was incredibly windy and we were blown through Central Park. The trees were beautiful in their September colours. We came out of Central Park on the corner by The Plaza opposite 5th Avenue to look in Tiffany's at the window displays. George was very thoughtful and was singing Sinead O'Connor's 'Nothing Compares to You', quietly, over and over.

Wearing a trench coat, beret and Doc Martin boots, ideal for doing a lot of walking in a gale but not great for posh shop shopping, I was dragged into Tiffany's, into the lift and up to the 2nd floor.

There was a Bell Boy in the elevator and he asked "Which floor?"

George replied, "Engagement rings."

I nearly fainted, I was pretty hot anyway.

A butler came over and we ordered champagne.

"Have you been in here before?" I asked.

"Yesterday afternoon whilst you were in the bath I nipped out and into here."

A charming gentleman appeared with four rings on a tray, together with the champagne foil paper wedding band.

"Oh, I see," I said, "that was clever of you."

George had chosen four rings for me to choose from, consequently saving me the worry of hoping not to choose one that was ridiculously expensive.

I gulped back the champagne, tried on all four rings, and said that I liked the first one. Everyone smiled because as it turned out that was the one that George liked best.

It was a square diamond with smaller diamonds surrounding the square and on the sides of the band.

The man from Tiffany's looked aghast at the state of my hands, at least I'd managed to remove most of the paint from under my unmanicured nails.

George said, "I'm going to put you in a cab back to the hotel now whilst I wait for the little blue box."

And this he did and we had a long lingering kiss on the street outside Tiffany's.

We were very quiet with each other in the hotel, we just couldn't stop smiling and frankly I was wondering where the ring was.

George had booked an evening dinner cruise departing from The World Yacht Marina, Pier 81 West 41st Street on a boat named 'The Duchess' on the

Hudson River.

It was a foggy night with drizzling rain. We couldn't see the Manhattan skyline and it was very damp. I was wearing a nineteen sixties black velvet midi dress and was missing my trench coat and beloved Doc Martins, when the cocktails arrive.

We sat down for dinner and after pudding, George slipped out for a cigarette as we turned under Brooklyn Bridge.

When he came back from the top deck, he asked me to return up there with him. I said no thank you because I can get all the fog and damp I need at home.

"You must come up and see the skyline," he said.

"Oh well, if you're sure there is one," I grumbled and grabbed my inadequate little bolero jacket.

I joined him in a cigarette. It is rare that I smoke and I felt like Lauren Bacall to his Humphrey Bogart as George hands me my lit cigarette and says in a very bad American accent, "Here's looking at you kid."

Suddenly the fog clears and the whole skyline is visible. The Manhattan skyline was on one side and behind it was the Statue of Liberty.

The weather was still blowing a gale and there were lots of Japanese tourists taking photographs. They were all giggling a lot and having fun. It was a lovely atmosphere.

I was admiring their tenacity and taking in the magnificent vista whilst enjoying my Marlborough Light when I turned to say something to George and I couldn't see him, I was concerned he'd fallen overboard when I realised he was down on one knee.

It's a bit like when I call for Blythe and the little dog is standing next to me all the while.

George threw his cigarette to the wind, grabbed my hand and I threw my cigarette away and hoped it wouldn't blow back because I know what's coming, obviously.

He held both of my hands in his and said. "Marry me, I love you, I need you, I can't be without you."

And with that, he started to cry with the emotion of it all. The Japanese tourists went quiet and were all smiling at us.

I wiped my own tears away and said, "I will marry you."

And we hugged, kissed, and jumped up and down as one does, but George was so overwhelmed I had to ask him where the ring was. He said, "Oh yes," and retrieved it from his jacket pocket and put it on my finger, it was a perfect fit thanks to the ring of gold foil template.

The jazz band began playing 'As Time Goes By' and we had our first ever proper dance together.

The other diners applauded as champagne was delivered to our table and George shouted, "She said yes."

One day after the engagement, five days away in total we flew back home on a Boeing Triple 7 with a free upgrade to club class because of George's contacts.

Our wedding was to be the first at Pemberton House and everyone joked at how good it was of us to show such dedicated commitment by trialling out the new wedding venue. However, for an early October wedding we had to get a move on.

Not only did we not want to wait but also we knew how busy we were going to be as bookings had started to come in.

If I thought Felicity was excited about George and me going to New York together it was nothing compared to her reaction when George and I told her about our engagement and wedding.

Bette was thrilled and said that she would like to come with me to choose my wedding outfit. In fact, we all made a day of it in London, travelling down together on the train and when we arrived at Euston George, Jack and Ben went off shopping for their clothes and Bette, Felicity and I went to Liberty's Vintage Rooms where we spent hours, it was delightful. I bought a Chanel suit, hat, and silk corsage in black and white. Bette found a beautiful hat, jacket, and Felicity looked gorgeous in a red crepe Ossie Clark dress with a little cape.

We then referred to Bette's planned itinerary and hailed a black cab to other vintage emporiums where we bought some platform shoes for Felicity that went perfectly with her dress and a little clutch bag and shoes for myself and Bette along with lots of accessories that none of us actually needed but had to have.

We went to Covent Garden for lunch in the basement of an Italian Restaurant and then on to shop at L'Occitane for perfumes and Neal's Yard for oils and other delightful potions and then it was time to meet George, Jack and Ben back at Euston. We were all laden with bags but fortunately, Bette had insisted on travelling first class and had managed to get quite a good deal on a group ticket out of the rush hour. So the travelling was enjoyable too.

Bette had also booked a table at Clouds for dinner for all of us including Lindy Lou so the wonderful day continued into the night and will be a memory that I shall always treasure.

Of course, whilst at Pemberton House wedding preparations were in full swing changes were happening on Rotten Row.

It looked quite sad with all the for sale signs up. The local estate agent, Mr Overlyedge couldn't believe it, so seldom did any cottage in Rotten Row come up for sale let alone the whole row.

Laney's was the first to be sold, then Jane and Freddie Harveys, followed by Babs Smythe's and Jock's and lastly Lucy and Jeremy's.

They were all sold within a period of twelve weeks, Mr. Overlyedge was rubbing his hands together gleefully and for Rotten Row a whole new era began.

My lovely Black Bird cottage was rented out quite quickly to a sweet young couple who were just starting out in their respective careers, she a teacher and her young husband a town planner. I just hoped they were up to the inquisitiveness of Elspeth.

Laney's new life in Brighton was keeping her busy and we planned to visit her in the summer as soon as we could. Jane and Freddie gave me their forwarding address and promised to come to the wedding. They were loving their new jobs and Shropshire.

Jock was very content in his mews house in Hampstead, was seeing quite a lot of Rosalind and Mark in London, and could hardly wait for the boat trips during the summer months.

Removal day for Lucy and Jeremy was hilarious with chickens going walkabout and having to dismantle the garden of canes, nets, dolly tubs, bins and other things used for container growing. I was there helping with Rosalind and I couldn't believe that such a tiny cottage could hold so much stuff, I don't think that they ever threw anything away.

It was a bright but cold day, we had a brazier going in the yard, and there is nothing like a hot cup of tea outside when you've been working.

There was laughter and tears. Leaving a home that you've loved is sad, but as I said to Jeremy and a very tearful Lucy. "You'll love your new home too, we're only ever caretakers of buildings you know, and these old places will still be here long after we've gone."

Rosalind came round with some whisky to put in the tea and some early mince pies. "May as well," she said. "Halloween and Christmas are in the shops at the same time, I've made pumpkin soup for later."

The move was being done in a horse box and Jock and Mark were up at the new cottage unloading, they were both staying at Rosalind's for the weekend to help out, so it was all hands on deck and a fun day all working together.

It was strange really, everyone thought of Lucy and Jeremy as young, in their twenties, but of course, they weren't at all but nonetheless people, not least, Rosalind who treated them as such and generally did things for them. Not a bad persona to adopt, being hopeless, however they were genuine.

But as Rosalind frequently said, "It's just how they are, quite useless at some things. They couldn't organise a piss up in a brewery, bless them, but they rear healthy chickens and grow great vegetables and their jams and Damson gin is well, stupendous! And of course they haven't got an ounce of badness in them, sometimes I wish that they had, they're just not very worldly and I don't know how that happened , having me for a mother. Both of them employed in jobs that required little thinking and were poorly paid yet they'd both had good educations, but they're happy and healthy and that's the most important thing."

We had more tea without the whisky due to loading and driving the horsebox and other laden cars up the lane.

The little cottage took a weekend to clear and in-between times we all went down to The Funnel and Gullet for pies and ale.

The hens were very happy as Rosalind had bought

and installed a new hen house for them and had had a new run built. The old one was dismantled and burnt on the brazier with the non-burnable bits taken to the nearest tip. Thank heaven for the horsebox. So Lucy, Jeremy and the hens now installed in their new home I returned to mine. Before I got into my van, I walked over the green and I stood outside Black Bird Cottage and silently thanked the little building for keeping Elvira, Blythe and me safe and said my goodbyes. I knew I wouldn't live there again; it was a part of my life that was over. Although I still owned Black Bird Cottage, it was no longer my home and my relationship with this small and cosy house had changed, like friends who move on.

I wiped the tears away as I saw Elspeth hurtling towards me. I had managed to avoid Elspeth for ages so she didn't know the details about my new life and I knew now that I was about to be asked a barrage of questions. I wasn't wrong.

She waved my wedding invitation under my nose.

"I do hope you and Charles can come," I said. "Matthew and his new partner Giovanni are coming; in fact they're staying at the venue."

"How long has this been going on," she asked, like an angry lover or partner.

"Oh, not long," I replied looking all innocent and a little vacant.

"Marry in haste, repent at leisure," she said, still waving the invitation about.

"Well I suppose I should be grateful that anyone should want me that isn't desperate, mad or a letch," I said, looking thoughtful.

"Who is your intended, how old is he, what does he do?" she hissed without drawing breath. Then she spotted my engagement ring and her mouth fell unattractively open.

"The name of my intended is on your invitation to our wedding. He is old enough and he is employed as a pilot. I'd also like to point out that pilots are checked out regularly to ensure that they are not mad and obviously, his eyesight is okay."

"Have you met my tenants, your new neighbours yet?" I asked, trying to change the subject.

"No, they've always been out when I've called round."

"Well they're young and just starting out in their careers so it's best not to disturb them."

"That's just what Charles said," replied Elspeth.

"Well, Charles knows best," I said. "I really must be going."

"Have you heard about Mrs Smythe?" asked Elspeth, desperate for a gossip.

"No, what?"

"She's broken her leg, in Spain."

"There are some who would say it should have been her neck," I replied, thinking of how badly she'd treated Laney and others in Rotten Row.

"Well it's not as simple as that, you see, Declan Kelly was flying out to join her, to live with her actually, he's been sacked from his job and he owes so many people lots of money because of his gambling and drink addiction."

"Tell me something I don't know," I said.

Elspeth continued, "Anyway, Mrs Smythe said she'd meet him at the airport," and at this point Elspeth's face broke out into a most uncharitable smile, thoroughly unbecoming for the wife of a vicar.

"She fell out of the taxi at the airport, drunk, bottle in hand and without paying for the taxi, stumbled into the arrivals section, bumping into everyone and everything as she went on her way to find the loo. She managed to lock the door and then immediately wet herself, the urine trickled under the door under the sandals of the angry taxi driver who was demanding to be paid and she couldn't get out. It was then that the swearing, kicking and banging started. In a desperate attempt to climb over the door she stood on the loo, fell off and broke her leg. Squeals of agony now joined the swearing and banging whilst airport staff and the fire brigade cut into the door to release her. A policeman had attempted to climb over the top of the door but she was impossible to help. By all accounts, she was in a terrible state. She was arrested and taken off to hospital but not before Declan had arrived, also drunk and then tried to rescue Mrs Smythe from the arms of the ambulance men and the police. Consequently, he was arrested too. Babs left in an ambulance and Declan in a police van; both were still making a racket. There was nothing wrong with the lock she was just too drunk to turn it the right way."

"How do you know all this?" I asked.

"Ah well, it's a small world isn't it and the Lord moves in mysterious ways."

"So you had a text message or an email from God then?"

"Don't be silly Louisa, the ladies of the flower guild told me."

"And how did those flower and church cleaning, brass rubbing uncharitable, rota obsessed harpies manage that? Were they actually there, in Spain?" I asked, smiling.

I liked to smile a beautific smile whilst being bitchy; it mirrored Elspeth and confused her.

"Yes, they were there to attend an arranged tour of

Spanish churches."

"What a bonus!" I exclaimed. "Such brilliant timing! Did any of them think to take a photo?"

"They did think about it but thought better of it being in the airport, they didn't want to be arrested as well."

"Where are Babs and Declan now?" I asked.

"No one knows, but apparently, Daisy, Declan's daughter, has flown out to Spain to be with her daddy."

"Thanks so much for that entertaining snippet of news, Elspeth. I can't wait to tell Laney and Rosalind and well just about everyone really."

"So Elspeth, the next time I shall see you will be at our wedding."

"I can't believe everything has changed so much," she replied.

"But life is ever changing Elspeth, nothing stands still."

Elspeth gave a disparaging glance at a bunch of teenagers who walked past us with all the energy of sedated sloths.

"You can't tell me that's a change for the better," she said.

I silently agreed. The group consisted of barely dressed young women pawed by dead eyed adolescents who needed to pull their trousers up.

"There's probably a private party at the Funnel and Gullet, one of them was carrying a brightly wrapped gift, anyway I understand it's quite fashionable to dress like a street worker, the sluttier the better with shoes that have heels so high they are impossible to walk in ensuring the derrière sticks out like that of a baboon."

"That's fashion for you," I said and swiftly changed the subject again.

"You'll have lots of new neighbours to meet soon; I understand from Mr Overlyedge that all of the sales are going through quite speedily. He was very chipper when I saw him the other day. He's looking after the rental of Black Bird cottage for me. Did you know?"

"I wonder what the new owners' reasons for buying were," I mused, "could their reasons have been as mixed as the sellers of Rotten Rows Cottages?

Jock is finally moving on from the past and relocating to London to enjoy friends and venues. The Harveys are taking live-in teaching jobs and buying a holiday cottage in Wales. Babs Smythe is moving out because of embarrassment at her lewd, drunken behavior and Laney a broken love affair resulting in a total life change.

And me in Black Bird Cottage, across the green, to love, marriage and a new career and family.

You don't have to be young to be starting out in life, there is always starting over," I said, dreamily.

"Is that what you're doing, starting over yet again, it's not as if you're that young anymore is it?" stated a very fed up looking Elspeth.

"Precisely, that's my point. I'm not young anymore but I'm happier than I've ever been and besides ageing is a privilege not a predicament, like anything else, it's how you deal with it. I must go now, Elspeth, I'll see you next week at Pemberton House for the wedding."

And with that, I started the engine of my trusted Acadiane Citroen van and drove away to my new life.

CHAPTER 17

The End and The Beginning

The wedding was delightful, a wonderful, wonderful day.

George had brought the wedding rings from Tiffany's as a surprise for me. Mine was a half band of diamonds to compliment my engagement ring and George's was plain white gold but for one discreet and tiny square diamond.

George was quite pleased with his bold ingenuity and so was I.

Ollie and Christo's flower creations were absolutely beautiful.

Jack had arranged the delicious food and the wedding cake.

Ben, a keen photographer took lots of photographs, as did all of the guests and this worked well because we wanted to keep the photographs informal and fun.

After the ceremony, we all went outside to have photographs taken on the steps of Pemberton House and Jack had driven George's red 1958 Jaguar XK150 "S" Roadster round to the front of the house to be the wedding car for the photographs, and because of this an extraordinary thing occurred.

Rosalind shrieked, dropped her handbag and exclaimed, "It's my car, my beloved car."

She then threw herself across the bonnet in raptures of uncharacteristic delight.

George cleared his throat to get her attention and said, "Actually it's my car.'"

Mark and Jock were looking not a little perplexed. Had the capable Rosalind that they knew and loved taken leave of her senses?

"Louisa, Louisa," she shouted. "You've married my car!"

And then the penny dropped.

"I haven't been imagining things after all; this car was driven past my house late at night and some very early mornings."

George explained that it was us just checking on Black Bird Cottage and promised Rosalind that she could drive her car again.

It was an emotional day.

The wedding music, chosen by George that I walked into the ballroom with, was West Life's 'This Love is Unbreakable'. I very nearly dissolved into a puddle of tears, which isn't bad for a John Lee Hooker sort of girl.

Felicity was an attentive bridesmaid and kept saying. "Don't cry Auntie, you'll look a mess."

Elvira and Blythe were escorting Bette and looked charming in their new felt coats and collars. The people we both loved were all there for us, the registrar was beaming and despite black looks from Elspeth, she did a splendid job. Charles, thrilled to have a day off and relieved not to have had the complexities of getting permissions from his bishop for two divorced people to marry, was really enjoying himself.

Jack was George's best man and together with Ben, they recited some readings from the book 'A Toltec The Four Agreements' by Don Miguel Ruiz.

Toltec knowledge arises from the same essential unity of truth as all the sacred esoteric traditions found around the world. Though it is not a religion, it honours all the spiritual masters who have taught on the earth. While it does embrace spirit, it is most accurately described as a way of life, distinguished by the ready accessibility of happiness and love.

The title of the following reading resulted in a few giggles directed at George and Elspeth's mouth turning downwards.

Prayer for Freedom

Today Creator of the Universe, we ask that you come to us and share with us a strong communion of love. We know that your real name is Love, that to have a communion with you means to share the same vibration, the same frequency that you are, because you are the only thing that exists in the universe.

Today help us to be like you are, to love life, to be life, to be love. Help us to love the way you love, with no conditions, no expectations, no obligations, without any judgement, because when we judge ourselves, we find ourselves guilty and we need to be punished.

Help us to love everything you create unconditionally, especially other human beings, especially those who live around us, all our relatives and people whom we try so hard to love. Because when we reject them, we reject ourselves, and when we reject ourselves we reject you.

Help us to love others just the way they are with no conditions. Help us to accept them the way they are, without judgement, because if we judge them, we find them guilty, we blame them, and we have the need to punish them.

Today, clean our hearts of any emotional poison that we have, free our minds from any judgement so that we can live in complete peace and complete love.

Today is a very special day. Today we open our hearts to love again so that we can tell each other "I love you," without any fear, and really mean it.

Today, we offer ourselves to you. Come to us, use our voices, use our eyes, use our hands, and use our hearts to share ourselves in a communion of love with everyone.

Today, Creator, help us to be just like you are.

Thank you for everything that we receive this day, especially for the freedom to be who we really are.

Amen.

I noticed that Matthew was wiping away his tears and so were a few of our other friends.

The reception went on into the early hours but everyone who stayed at Pemberton House was up surprisingly early for a hearty breakfast and a walk around the grounds.

Our trip to New York served as our honeymoon in advance and on the following Monday after our wedding, it was back to work.

George was back flying and Pemberton House was getting really busy.

With Felicity's summer trolley dolly contract at its end she decided with a little persuasion to take on marketing and public relations courses with a view to helping us run Pemberton House and a few other ventures we all had in mind.

Ben proposed to Felicity and the engagement party was at Clouds restaurant with the wedding planned at Pemberton House, though the ceremony was to take place in the nearby St Mary's Church.

When they first moved in together and she was studying, she rang me excitedly one day to tell me that Ben had given her their first months housekeeping money and she had just returned from shopping. With the housekeeping, she had bought an Indian chest of drawers and said that although it was a ghastly shade of green she was off down to the garage to distress it to put it with a lovely mirror that she had found and was also working on.

George said. "Like Auntie, like niece."

I have heard the quote, 'Find something you like doing and do it for the rest of your life.'

Now I have and I'm so fortunate to be doing just that, it's never too late to try a different path and hopefully love the people along it.

Who knows, this could be the nicest life I've ever had and I've had a few.

THE END.

3321338R00136

Printed in Great Britain
by Amazon.co.uk, Ltd.,
Marston Gate.